WHITE ORCHID

When successful young writer and artist Kate Summers boarded that tiny plane, she hoped for a pleasant working holiday at the Wiatapi Guest Lodge in Papua, New Guinea — a holiday blessedly free of men, and memories of the past. Instead, she found herself in a terrifying situation — and dependant upon one man for her very survival. But how far could she trust the dark and enigmatic Matt Selby — and worse, how far could she trust her own feelings for him?

DINA McCALL

WHITE ORCHID

Complete and Unabridged

LINFORD
Leicester

First published in Great Britain in 1988 by
Robert Hale Limited
London

First Linford Edition
published 1999
by arrangement with
Robert Hale Limited
London

British Library CIP Data

McCall, Dina
    White orchid.—Large print ed.—
    Linford romance library
    1. Love stories
    2. Large type books
    I. Title
    823.9′14 [F]

    ISBN 0–7089–5582–7

Published by
F. A. Thorpe (Publishing) Ltd.
Anstey, Leicestershire

Set by Words & Graphics Ltd.
Anstey, Leicestershire
Printed and bound in Great Britain by
T. J. International Ltd., Padstow, Cornwall

This book is printed on acid-free paper

1

The tearing and crashing had stopped, and an uneasy silence fell over the forest. The small twin-engined Otter lay mangled amongst the branches, for all the world like a white moth impaled on a pin. It hung precariously, one wing and part of the fuselage missing, the other wing reaching down towards the thick undergrowth. Two hundred feet above it, the dark green canopy of the rain forest showed no sign of its violent entry, as though the mengaris trees had swallowed it whole in one indifferent gulp. A bird of paradise darted past, jewel-bright, intent on its own business. A brown tree-snake, disturbed by the plane's intrusion, slithered smoothly towards it, and then hesitated. Something there had moved. Something was alive.

Kate Summers groaned and stirred in her seat, stretching long legs. Her chest hurt. A deep breath. Painful. Her head felt fuzzy too. Her cheek was pressed against something folded and placed there to support her head — a man's jacket. Gingerly, she turned. The seat next to her was empty. She felt a rush of relief. The man had gone, that man who had stared at her so when she was boarding the plane. If only she didn't feel so confused!

She closed her eyes. The plane . . . she could remember the internal flight across Australia from Sydney to Darwin. She could see herself clearly, walking out into the hard sunlight of Darwin airport, crossing the hot tarmac to board the tiny chartered plane that would carry her on the last phase of her journey to Papua, New Guinea.

But then, it became hazy. She remembered seeing the man. There had been the sickening shock of recognition, seeing that broad back in its khaki shirt, the arrogant shoulders, the black hair . . . David . . . !

But the man had turned, and revealed a different face. Not David at all . . . how stupid of her, after all this time . . . a perfect stranger.

Kate groaned. She opened her eyes, but it was too gloomy to make out more than dim shapes. She was tipped uncomfortably over to one side, still held in her seat by the restraining belt. Perhaps that was why her chest hurt.

The fact that the plane must have crashed, she seemed able to accept without too much difficulty. Strangely, it was the memory of the man that disturbed her. When she was boarding the plane, he had stared at her. Not surprising, perhaps, the way she had been gawping at him, but his scrutiny made her nervous. She'd pretended to adjust her shoulder bag, looking for her sunglasses, settling them on her nose with shaking fingers, smoothing back her mane of hair that was the colour of pale dry sherry. Then she had swept past him with a swirl of her coloured skirt and a confidence she did not feel, and followed the other passengers into the plane. She'd gone right to the back, choosing the last seat of all, hoping to be inconspicuous. But he had followed her.

Or probably, she'd told herself as she settled herself and her belongings, he was not following her at all. He just liked sitting at the rear of planes — lots of people did. And he had nothing to do with David. He did not even look like him . . . not really, even though something about him still seemed oddly familiar. David had been handsome, and this man was hardly that. His face was too broad, with its high flat cheekbones, and his hair too black and coarse. Why then worry that he had chosen to sit beside her?

She'd stared fixedly out of the window, while the final passengers boarded. The engines had roared

4

into life, they began to taxi along the runway. She had not been aware that she was clenching her fists, until he spoke to her.

'There's no need to be scared. I've taken this trip many, many times. Just relax.'

A pleasant voice, deeper than David's, and with a slight American intonation . . . no similarity to upset her there. But there was an assurance about it, a brusque kindliness that said he thought himself sitting beside one of those stupid women who might become hysterical, and was trying to save himself the nuisance of it.

'I can assure you, I am not in the least bit scared,' she'd returned coldly, and had continued to stare out until they rose sharply and left the airport far behind.

★ ★ ★

Kate groaned again, and made the effort to concentrate. This wasn't

Darwin airport. Where the hell was she?

The fuzziness began to recede. Memories became clearer, and panic sidled in with the returning clarity. She could remember now what had followed. The plane . . . the man . . . rousing out of a doze to find him leaning across her, his face close to hers, his hand warm and heavy on her knee. Fright had made her voice shrill.

'What d'you think you're doing?'

He had turned, not a bit put out by her breathless outrage, eyes black and piercing, hair flopping forward over his forehead, a khaki shirt open at the collar showing a neck that was brown and set strongly on the wide shoulders. The sheer animal magnetism of him hit her suddenly, making her stare in bewilderment that was not entirely due to having been so rudely awakened.

'Fasten your belt . . . here.' He had taken it roughly and clipped her in. As his hand touched hers she'd recoiled, but then she'd become aware that

6

things were happening, things that had nothing to do with this man, or the way he made her feel. A woman in front started complaining in a high querulous voice. 'What's going on?' Other voices joined in.

'Don't panic . . . ' someone shouted. The obvious note of alarm had the opposite effect. Kate realized that in her sleep she had missed what had disturbed them. A startled glance out of the window at a sea of dark green forest rushing to meet them and she'd known what was missing. She could not hear the engines.

The next moment they tipped violently forward . . . and the screaming started. The man grabbed her. This time she did not object. She buried her face in the soft linen of his shirt, her hands clutching at him, his arms tight about her. A jarring impact . . . being torn from his arms and shaken about like a rag doll . . . her own voice high pitched and terrified . . . and then blackness . . . and at last, oblivion.

She was in bed, in her flat in Sydney . . . She knew she must be, but something was wrong, very wrong. Yet, what could it possibly be?

It had been a very good season for Kate. She'd finished the illustrations for her children's picturebook, *The Land of the Waugal*, in good time and it had been well received. The initial publicity had been good, even in Australia where she had expected they might be more than critical of a mere 'Pom' having the temerity to write about their aboriginal myths and legends.

Evan, who was her agent and therefore had a financial interest in her success, was pleased too. Perhaps that wasn't being fair to him. He was genuinely pleased for her on a more personal level. He'd have taken their relationship further, if she'd let him, but so far, with some difficulty, she had managed to keep things on a purely friendly basis. And that was how she wanted it to remain.

It was Evan who had suggested a more serious exhibition of paintings in Sydney, to coincide with publication of her book. He had arranged it all, and had even travelled with her from London to set it up, and that was unusual. Evan didn't generally put himself out to such an extent, even for his most important clients. And this made things difficult, thought Kate. She was fond of him, but she had no intention of becoming romantically involved with him . . . or with any man. She had been hurt once . . . and once was more than enough.

Evan had seen her well and truly launched into the exhibition with its attendant publicity. It had been an exciting and important project . . . important to her career, and so she could understand his feelings of annoyance when she dropped the bombshell that she was off once again — this time to New Guinea.

'But what on earth for?' he demanded. His face had turned quite pink.

They were enjoying an intimate dinner for two at Gino's, a small Italian restaurant tucked away in a back street in the older, picturesque part of Sydney. Kate had been reluctant to accept his invitation, feeling that he was becoming too serious for her peace of mind — but it had been hard to refuse . . . he had been so kind, and had helped her so much. Why, she wondered ruefully, did men get romantic notions about her? Quite frankly, she couldn't see it. She was nothing special to look at, no bosomy blonde, or sultry brunette — just a rather tall, willowy girl with high cheekbones, eyes that sometimes seemed blue and sometimes darkened to a haunted violet, depending on her mood, and thick crinkly blonde hair that stood out in a halo around her face. If anything, it was her hair that made her unusual. Evan said she looked like a woman in a Pre-Raphaelite painting, with that pale mass of refractory waves.

Well, be that as it may, she wished it did not have such an annoying effect on him. She knew too well where it would lead. You let yourself fall in love . . . you trusted and gave your whole heart to someone . . .

Never again! Kate finished off the last spoonful of pavlova with relish, licking away a crumb of meringue from the corner of her mouth. She smiled at Evan affectionately. 'I want to start collecting material for my next book,' she said hoping to mollify. 'While I'm in the mood. While I still feel enthusiastic about it. If I leave it much longer I might lose impetus.'

'But you ought to be here . . . at your exhibition . . . Surely you can see that.'

He was very earnest. His grey eyes held hers with almost dog-like devotion. It worried her. She wished he wouldn't, she preferred him when he was his usual decisive self.

'I don't really need to be there in person now,' she protested. 'At the beginning, yes. But the interest is tailing off, and it's time I was on my way. New Guinea will give me a new exhibition.' She leaned forward, wrinkling her nose at him, blue eyes coaxing. 'Don't be cross with me. D'you think I could have a coffee?'

Diverted, he ordered, and she watched him with a slight frown. He was quite good-looking, in a mature, distinguished way: hair going grey and a little thin, discreetly combed across. He was a kind man, and gentle. He had even hinted that he wanted to marry her; sometimes she felt pleased about it, but more often she simply felt confused. If she were ever to marry anyone she would as soon it was him. She perhaps would be safe with him. Safe from hurt.

The coffee arrived, and he stubbornly returned to his theme. 'But why so soon?' He looked at her shrewdly. 'It isn't anything to do with me, is it?'

Unnerved at the way he had read her thoughts, Kate gulped at her drink too quickly, scalding her lips. The black coffee slopped into her saucer. 'They fill the cups too full,' she complained, wiping her fingers on her napkin. But Evan was too perceptive to be fooled.

'You know what I'm talking about. There are times when I can't fathom you out. Did you see the review in *Mode Australia*? 'This artist offers an intriguing conflict of styles. Her pen sketches of aboriginal faces have a cool, pure, almost clinical exactitude . . . whereas her abstracts explode in a sensuous passion of colour. Just which, we wonder, is the real Kate Summers?' '

He leaned back in his chair. 'I often ask myself the same question. You've told me very little about your life before I met you.'

He was digging, but fond of him though she was Kate had no intention of satisfying his curiosity. There were some areas of her life she could never share. She glanced at her watch pointedly. 'There isn't much to tell.

And what there is would only bore you. I'm sorry . . . but if I'm to fly tomorrow I must get back to my packing.'

He took the hint, and changed the subject, talking instead about her intended stay at Wiatapi. He had stayed there once. Set in the foothills, not far from Port Moresby, it was not too hot and humid. A fascinating variety of tribes could be found in the area, and it would be easy to arrange expeditions into the forest to the native villages which would surely provide her with plenty of inspiration for both book and paintings.

She was grateful to him for his tact, and by the time they reached the door of the apartment she had rented for the duration of the exhibition, she was feeling so indulgent towards him that she even invited him in for a nightcap.

'Are you sure?' he queried, only half teasing. She paused, startled to hear an unusual note of sarcasm in his voice.

'Of course,' she faltered, suddenly

unsure as she unlocked the door. Evan had always seemed so predictable. He wasn't going to go all temperamental on her now, was he? No, of course not. 'Make yourself at home . . . pour yourself a drink. I'm going to have another coffee so that I can stay awake to do my packing.'

She discarded the light jacket she was wearing over a blue silk sleeveless dress that complemented the colour of her eyes, and kicked off her high-heeled sandals, wandering barefoot into the tiny kitchen while Evan slid open the long french windows, and took his drink onto the balcony. The coffee made, she joined him, cup in hand. The apartment overlooked Sydney harbour, and now, in the soft warm darkness, the lights of the city were spread out below them. A breeze, wafting in the scent of eucalyptus, caressed her bare arms already tanned by the strong Australian sun.

She liked it here. She had no real desire to move on, but it was best. She didn't want Evan to fall in love with her. Not really . . . or perhaps, more to the point, she didn't want to fall in love with him. Kate shivered.

'Cold?' asked Evan.

She laughed briefly. 'No . . . someone walked over my grave, I expect!'

All the same Evan stepped back inside, and Kate followed him, closing the windows with a feeling of unease. She had never felt so over-awake, so tense and edgy. She shouldn't have had that last coffee . . . serve her right for trying to distract Evan. She knew she was running away from the situation, but she didn't want to be pinned down to either rejecting or accepting him. She really was extremely fond of him . . . but was that enough?

As if sensing that he was the object of her thoughts, he reached out his arms. For a moment she hesitated, wanting to turn away, but then leaned against him, her head on his shoulder.

'I suppose I'm far too old for you!' he said with a sigh.

Kate laughed. 'Old . . . you? What rubbish!'

'I'm forty-six. Twenty years older than you.'

'So what? I hardly want a teenager for an agent. Maturity and experience, that's what counts.'

For once she could not turn him. 'You know perfectly well what I'm talking about, Kate.'

She paid him the compliment of not trying to pretend, dropping her arms back to her sides. It was a gesture with a hint of weariness in it. 'If I ever do marry it will probably be to you.' Even as she admitted it, she felt trapped. 'But I'm not ready for that, Evan,' she added hurriedly, unaware that her reluctance showed so clearly on her expressive face. 'Can't we just remain good friends?'

'Kate!'

He pulled her to him, and kissed her, his mouth demanding.

She tried to respond, but as his passion rose her panic flared up. So

17

stupid . . . even with dear, harmless Evan! Why was she like this? As Evan's lips pressed against hers her heart pounded up into her throat . . . she could not breathe. Straining away from him she pushed her hands flat against his chest.

'*No!* Evan . . . let me go!'

He ignored her, and she began to struggle, eyes wide, her breathing fast. 'Evan, please!'

He released her. 'Where is the sensuous, passionate Kate that is revealed in her paintings?' His lips twisted wryly. 'I never see her.'

'You're talking nonsense,' she protested, laughing in an effort to defuse a situation which had become intolerably intense. A hot flush rose in her cheeks. 'You of all people should know better than to take publicity seriously. And anyway,' her voice faltered, 'you know I hate to be mauled about.'

'Mauled!' He was angry. This in itself was so unusual that Kate stiffened, but then he stepped back from her, his face

18

serious. 'I take *you* seriously. You're right, Kate. You need to get away on your own. Perhaps you can sort yourself out at Wiatapi. Goodness knows, you're a mess . . . '

'Evan!'

She had thought him a rock — someone she could depend upon, reliable and . . . well yes, blessedly unemotional. Unlikely to want more than she could give. It shook her to find how wrong she could be. 'How can you say that?' she blurted in dismay. 'You told me I had never painted better . . . '

He dismissed what she was saying with an impatient wave of his hand. 'Oh, career-wise, yes . . . you are highly successful. And likely to go on being so. But *you*, Kate — the real you inside — you're a tangled mess of inhibitions. God knows what or who did it to you. I thought I could help, but you won't let me near.' He put his hands on her shoulders, and kissed her lightly on her forehead. 'Off you go, Kate, and see if you can't find yourself.'

She felt suddenly bereft. 'You . . . you're returning to London?'

He nodded. 'But don't worry. I'll be waiting, when you return. *If* you want me.' He smiled, a little sadly. 'Don't get me wrong, Kate. I want you, but not in the cold-blooded way you seem to imagine — I'm not that old yet. I've no intention of being a father figure.'

That stung. She had adored her father, but in no way was she looking for a substitute. 'I wouldn't want you to be,' she flared. 'I don't know what's the matter with you, Evan. You seem to have developed some funny ideas about me.'

'Have I?' He shrugged. 'The critics were right. Cold, pure and clinical. You like to feel safe with a man, don't you? Like to have him in a nice antiseptic little box . . . well, men aren't like that. As you'll find out one of these days.'

'I think you've said enough,' said Kate stiffly. 'Perhaps you'd better go now.'

Evan nodded. 'I'll see you when you

get back, my dear. And if you feel the same, don't worry. As your agent I make a lot of money out of you, my child!'

After he had gone Kate closed the door, and leaned her forehead against it for a moment. 'Damn!' she muttered vehemently, pounding it softly with a closed fist. She didn't want to lose Evan. She *needed* him. He was all she had; the only person at all close to her. Why couldn't he be content with things as they were? Or, equally well, why couldn't she give him the response he wanted? But she already knew the answer to that one.

She walked slowly into the bedroom. She slipped out of her dress and replaced it with a thin cotton robe, tying it about her slender waist. Then she sat on the single bed and allowed herself to fall back — stretching out, her hands behind her head, staring up at the featureless ceiling. She forced herself to think of mundane things: that, she had found from bitter experience, was the only way to cope with emotions one did not wish to examine, and she had no wish to examine hers right now.

Packing. That was what she must fix her mind on. With a muttered exclamation she sprang to her feet, and began flinging clothes into a bag, fiercely concentrating on them to the exclusion of all else. She would have to take trousers, though she did not like wearing them. She preferred clothes that were loose and comfortable, particularly here in the heat. Tomorrow, for travelling, she would wear her new wrap-around skirt with its bright primary colours, and a sleeveless white silk top that made her bare arms appear even browner. Some uncrushable dresses, to wear in the evenings, and a couple of bikinis — there was a pool at Wiatapi, she believed — and that was almost it.

At last, with a flurry of activity, she finished by zipping up the two soft-topped bags: one would travel as luggage, the other smaller one could stay with her in the plane. She had her notebook and sketch pad in that, plus a few other items she might need on the journey. Restlessly she padded about the apartment, refusing to face the questions that the evening had thrown up.

In desperation, she made a hot milky drink. That was what she needed. Never failed! In any case, tomorrow she would be far away, in quite a different world, and her problems would be behind her.

She tried to hold that thought later, as she tossed and turned in a bed that suddenly seemed too hot and too hard, and when she did finally doze off it was to uneasy dreams. Wrong . . . something was very, very wrong . . .

* * *

'Wake up . . . come on, wake up.'

The voice became insistent, breaking through her muddled thoughts. Kate's head threshed wildly on her pillow. But it wasn't her pillow, she suddenly realized. This wasn't her bed, her apartment. With a sinking feeling she knew she had returned from dreaming, to a reality worse than any nightmare. Hands held her by her shoulders, shaking, jerking her head backwards and forwards. She gave a moan of protest, and pushed at whoever it was that was treating her so roughly. Reluctantly, dreading what she would see, she opened her eyes.

A dark face was close to her own, eyes boring mercilessly into hers. He was crouching over her. She could feel the clutch of strong fingers, the warmth of his hands. David? No, not David . . . not ever again.

That's when Kate began to scream.

2

'Stop that!'

The voice was sharp, but the slap to her face was sharper, the shock of it painfully effective. The world swirled around Kate with a kaleidoscope of colours, and then focussed again as she hiccuped from her hysteria into uncontrollably shaking sobs. The face looking into hers was not David's. Not David's. She kept repeating that, holding on to sanity. It was dark, true, but it didn't have David's smooth good looks. It was a harsh face, with black penetrating eyes that were now holding hers, willing her into silence. How could she have made such a stupid mistake twice in quick succession. It was the man from the plane — he must be thinking her a complete idiot. Not that she cared what he thought.

'I'm . . . I'm sorry,' she gasped,

unable to stop the sobs that were racking her.

He moved away from her to undo her belt, and she immediately found herself sliding sideways into what appeared to be a tangle of leaves that intruded into the plane, blocking the rear from the rest. He caught her around the middle, and instinctively she began to struggle.

'Will you stop that?' he grunted, yanking her into a sitting position. She found herself leaning hard against him, his arms wrapped around her, supporting, rocking.

'Hush now. It's all right. You're safe.'

His voice was deep and reassuring, but still Kate strained against him, her body taut as a bow. Her hands fluttered ineffectually against his shirt. 'You can let go. Please — let me go.'

He released his grip slowly, almost reluctantly, as if not believing her, expecting her to relapse back into hysteria. Levering himself against the

26

nearest seat, he drew away into a squatting position. To Kate's heightened perception, even in the gloom of the plane's interior, his face seemed brutal in its tough outlines, black hair awry over his forehead, full lips clamped together. His dark eyes held her face, and then travelled downwards, deliberately examining her.

Why was he looking at her like that? Kate was only too aware that her wrap-around skirt was pulled up, showing naked smooth thighs, her sleeveless silk top, now soiled and sticky with the heat, clinging to her in a revealing manner. 'Sorry,' she apologised again hurriedly, her eyes flicking away from him in embarrassment. 'I'm not usually the screaming kind.'

He gave a short laugh. 'In the circumstances, I'll forgive you. It's the shock.'

Kate drew a quivering breath. 'Yes,' she agreed bleakly. 'You can say that again.' She pulled up her knees, dragging her skirt over them, anything to get further away from him. She looked around her, and when she did speak her voice was near enough normal.

'It's just . . . everything happened so fast.'

'Dirty fuel, I'd guess,' he said in a voice that had turned implacably hard. 'I'm willing to bet someone supplied low-grade stuff and pocketed the difference, instead of filling up at the airport. When we get out of this he'll be sorry.' He clenched his fists until his knuckles turned white.

Kate shivered in spite of the heat, and smoothed her hair away from her face. Her fingers felt shaky, rubbery. He sounded so sure of himself, so dangerous, she would hate to be anybody who fell foul of him. And yet she could not blame him for feeling vindictive. Who wouldn't?

'When I came to my senses the first time, you weren't there.' To her annoyance the remark sounded childishly accusing. Almost as if she had been angry at his desertion.

He shrugged. 'I checked you were alive. It seemed best to leave you strapped in. Safer that way.' His eyes travelled her again, flickering over her with an impersonal curiosity that made her squirm. 'You aren't hurt, are you?'

Without thinking Kate's hand flew to her chest. It was still sore, but not so painful when she breathed as it had been. 'No . . . I'm fine.'

He had been quick to see her gesture. 'Your chest hurts? Here, I'd better make sure nothing's broken.' Leaning forward he gripped her shoulders, his fingers pressing around her collar bone gently but firmly. Then one hand moved lower, over the white silk top, to feel down around her ribs. As his hand slid over the thin material a tidal wave of heat seared through her, making her catch her breath in her throat with a tiny guttural sound.

He had heard. For a moment he drew away from her, but his hand remained where it was. He stared at

29

her, but if he drew any conclusion from her trembling lips he did not show it. Deliberately he finished his examination.

'You're OK. Just some bruising.'

She was able to breathe again. Ignore it. He obviously was only trying to help. There were more important things to worry about than the strange effect he had had on her ever since she first clapped eyes on him. Survival was the only thing that mattered.

Deliberately she forced herself to look him in the face. 'So, when you left me unconscious, where were you?'

He nodded to where the sunlight splattered through the leaves. 'Checking to see if there was anyone else alive.'

'And was there?' He didn't need to answer. Nine others there had been besides themselves, not quite a full load, all bound for a holiday at Wiatapi Guest Lodge. There was that woman she had met in the airport lounge . . . and the boy, returning for a holiday with his parents. They were to have had

30

a break before returning to the copra plantation his father managed. Kate's eyes filled with tears.

'No use feeling sorry for yourself.'

The injustice steadied her. 'I'm not! I was only . . . '

'I know roughly where we are,' he continued. 'I got a brief check out of the window before we came down, and I could see the river. If we're near the top of the ridge, and I guess we are, then we're lucky. I reckon we're not all that far from Wiatapi. If we'd come down lower we wouldn't have stood an earthly. The jungle's so thick there we'd never get through.'

So that was what he had been doing when she had woken from her doze in the plane to find him leaning over her, his hand on her knee . . . and she had thought he was getting fresh! Mortified, Kate lashed herself for her vivid imagination.

'Big deal!' she said. He looked at her sourly. She knew she sounded belligerent, but it was the way he made her feel, treating her like a spoiled child. 'Is anyone likely to find us?' she continued.

He pulled himself up to his feet, and as he did so the whole plane rocked and Kate stifled a gasp of alarm.

'No,' he answered bluntly. 'From the air there won't be a sign. And we were slightly off-course. There was heavy cloud; the pilot tried to get above it, but one engine cut out and then the other. No, they won't be looking here.'

She had insisted on hearing the truth, but he could have been a bit more diplomatic about it! If he wanted to frighten her he had succeeded, but instead of making her feel worse it only made her angry with him as if their predicament was his fault, and that was a lot better than the way she'd been feeling up to now. She looked up at him, blue eyes dark with antagonism.

'Then what do you suggest we do?'

He turned his back on her. 'We walk out of here. I know this area.

Over the ridge and down the other side and we stand a good chance of reaching a native village.'

Having said that, he stopped, pushing his way through the foliage, into the other part of the plane, as though dismissing her. His broad shoulders blocked her view of what he was doing. Slowly, carefully, she rose to her feet and edged towards him. He was bending over someone. Suddenly a hand flopped down in front of her, and she recoiled, stifling a scream. He didn't say anything, and at last she summoned up the courage to speak.

'What are you doing?'

'Isn't it obvious?'

She edged nearer, and her heart lurched into her mouth.

He was . . . he was taking the clothes.

'Stop that!' she gasped. 'How dare you.' She hardly recognised her own outraged cry, or felt the blows she rained on his back. He turned, catching her by her wrists, his fingers biting into her flesh, and forced her hands down and then behind her.

'I'm walking out of here, lady. And if you want to get out of this alive, you're coming with me.' Impatience and scorn were obvious in his voice. 'How far d'you think you'd get dressed like that?' He jerked his head. 'He's not needing these now, poor devil, but you are. Give us a hand.'

Distasteful though it was, Kate could see the force of his reasoning. Biting her lip, she helped him to remove the strong denim jeans. Then he tucked a travelling blanket over the erstwhile owner, tenderly, almost reverentially. So he did have some feelings of compassion, after all.

'Here — get into them.'

Kate hesitated. 'Come on,' he snapped. 'It'll be dark very soon, and we must make a start. Get out of that flimsy thing and put these on.'

As she stood petrified he glanced at her, puzzled, and then gave a snort of exasperation. 'For goodness sake, girl.

34

D'you think I've never seen a woman before? You've got a pretty big opinion of yourself, haven't you?'

Kate flushed, and undid the fastening at her waist, letting her bright floral skirt drop away, until she stood before him, her long slender legs, brown and smooth, shapely thighs ending at a pocket-handkerchief-sized triangle of lace that clung to the swelling curve of her hips. He didn't even have the decency to turn his head, but watched her with dark appraisal. Feeling humiliated and ridiculous she put out her hand, and he gave her the trousers. She tugged them up, fumbling at the fastening.

'Here . . . let me.'

He took the belt and drew it tighter, his knuckles pressing against her waist. She averted her head, avoiding his eyes. It was too loose, and he felt in his pocket and brought out a knife with a spike, making a new hole in the leather. 'Now for the top.' He found her a jacket, of strong khaki material.

The sleeves were too long for her, and it felt hot. She told him so.

'That's the least of your worries, sweetheart. Better hot than bitten to death.'

Suddenly the whole situation seemed completely mad. '*Must* we do this?' Kate blurted, looking desperately around her. 'These were people . . . nice, kind, ordinary people.'

Hysteria was not far away, the shakiness of her voice betrayed it. To her surprise she found herself in his arms again. 'I know,' he said softly.

For a second she thought she felt his lips against her hair, but before her raw nerves made her recoil again he had pushed her away, and was busy rummaging through a black handbag that had spilled across the aisle. Her own painful confusion made her speak scathingly.

'And *now* what are you doing? I suppose they won't need their money either?'

She saw his back stiffen. 'Try not to be so stupid! Go through all the bags, pockets too. I can't get into the luggage hold, the doors have jammed. Collect anything that might be of use, matches, knives, food, any medicines. We might need them. Use your common sense . . . if you have any.'

Again he had made her feel a fool. Resentfully she did what she was told. As she searched, trying not to look too closely at the silent occupants of the seats, she wished with all her heart that she was once again waking up in her Sydney appartment.

Good heavens . . . it was hard to believe it had been that very morning. She had woken after a disturbed sleep, still annoyed with Evan. While getting ready to leave she had fumed, going over in her mind the events of the night before. She admired and respected him. Surely, if he was thinking of marriage such qualities were important. More important than so-called love, which she now knew was such a snare and delusion. But if he did not think it enough . . .

She had locked up the apartment, and dropped the key into her bag; the flat was to be kept on until it was time to pack up the exhibition. She had everything to look forward to. The last few years had been good. She had found a new confidence in herself. She was a success, and she had plans for other, more ambitious projects. A mess . . . huh! She had hailed a taxi, glad that Evan's own departure for London stopped him from seeing her off at the airport. She was used to being alone, preferred it, she told herself fiercely. Perhaps that was what was really riling Evan. They say men like helpless women, but being helpless was not her way, and she wasn't going to pretend to be so now in order to boost a male ego — not even dear Evan's!

'How are you doing back there?' The man's voice brought Kate back to the present. Her own reluctant search had not yielded much that was of use.

'So far I've found a penknife, a packet of biscuits, a tube of wine gums, a half-eaten apple, and some chocolate.'

'Not bad. Find a bag to put them in.'

She pushed her way precariously back to her own seat, and found her flight bag, blue leather with her monogrammed initials on it, and tipped out the contents. Make-up was not of prime importance here, she thought grimly, though the moistened cleaning tissues might be useful. She replaced her own things with those she had collected, and then feeling guilty, took back a couple of pencils and some sheets of paper. Having them was a habit she couldn't break.

She had been glad of them on the flight from Sydney to Darwin. No matter how much she travelled — and by any standards she had covered a fair part of the world in the last few years — she never lost the excitement of seeing a strange landscape spread like a map beneath her. If she had taken the direct route via the Cape York Peninsula she would have lost seeing much of Southern Australia and the Northern Territory, an opportunity she had not wanted to miss.

By the time they had arrived at Darwin she had quite a collection of thumb-nail studies of many of the passengers, working with quick, deft pencil-strokes, wondering with amusement whether any of them would be travelling on to Wiatapi with her. As it happened, they were not. That had not been surprising: the guest-house was quite exclusive, and not on the usual holiday-maker's circuit. It was more the retreat of the very rich who were seeking something different, or else people such as herself, with a more serious purpose in mind, anthropologists maybe, or botanists, who found it a convenient base.

Her anticipation had risen to a peak once she landed at Darwin and passed through the doors of the departure lounge to where the Guest Lodge's own little chartered aircraft was waiting to take the week's new arrivals on to New Guinea.

Kate paused in her packing, seeing herself striding across the airport tarmac pleasantly aware of the hot sun on her face, a breeze lifting her hair and whipping her skirt around her legs, eagerly studying the passengers who were gathering to travel with her. She had been relaxed, smiling . . . until she saw the man.

When he sat beside her she had tried to ignore him, and after that first remark of his, which she had so effectively snubbed, he had not ventured to speak to her again. All the same she had been awkwardly conscious of his long legs in immaculately pressed khaki linen trousers, his broad shoulders so close that at times his arm had brushed hers. She had not looked at him directly, but could not help noticing his hands, strong brown fingers turning the pages of a book he was engrossed in. He didn't appear at all conscious of her. Why should he be? A perfect stranger, not giving her a second thought, but all the time he was sitting there she felt she was holding her breath.

She had no idea why. It couldn't be because for one petrifying moment she had thought that he was David? No, it was the man himself, the way his eyes had caught hers while she was still standing on the airport tarmac; the blatant raw strength of him. She had felt it reaching out towards her, felt herself gripped by his gaze. It disturbed her.

'Have you finished?'

It was a shock to find herself back in the plane, with him beside her again. Mutely she held out her offerings. He took the chocolate, and broke it in half. 'It's going soft already. Better eat it now.'

He unwrapped his piece, and began to eat. She looked at him with disbelief.

'How can you . . . ?'

He licked one finger, and lifted a sardonic brow. 'Easy. I know how hungry we'll get. Take what you can when you can. Eat it.'

She shook her head angrily. Who did he think he was, to order her around in such an arrogant manner? He took the chocolate from her fingers, picked off the remains of the silver wrapping, and held it to her mouth. As she tried to turn her head away he pressed it against her lips, and it smeared them with its melting sweetness. She had no choice.

'Good girl.'

He fished in his pocket and pulled out a handkerchief, leaning forward to wipe her mouth. His touch scalded her, and she knocked away his hand, scarlet with rage.

'I can do it myself.'

He shrugged, and picked up a pair of walking shoes. 'Put these on. They may be a bit big, but here are some socks.'

Kate recoiled. 'Socks! I can't wear those.'

He sighed. 'I found them in the hand luggage,' he said patiently, as if he was talking to a difficult child. 'Now don't be silly. You wouldn't last a minute in sandals.'

'But how far is it, to the nearest native village?'

He thought a moment. 'About seven miles.'

Relief coursed through her veins. 'Is that all!' she said scornfully. 'I've often done that before breakfast.'

His glance was pitying. 'It'll take at least seven days through this jungle, if we're lucky. Lift up your foot.'

Once more he took charge of her, slipping the strappy sandal from her foot, sliding a sock over her high instep. She squirmed at the feel of his fingers, and he glanced up at her, a devil in his eyes, grinning sardonically, showing teeth that were strong and white.

'You don't half fancy yourself, d'you know? My God, I've known some jittery females in my time, but you take the biscuit.'

Her face flaming, Kate snatched the other sock from him, and put it on, pushing her feet into the shoes, lacing them up, her fears forgotten in a surge of temper.

'Not too bad a fit,' he remarked. 'Here, give us your bag. Might as well put these things into it as well.'

He had found a torch, a packet of sandwiches, some pain-killers, matches, and a flask that contained brandy. He packed it all into her bag, together with some large handkerchiefs. 'Might come in handy, if we need a bandage.'

Kate swallowed. What was it going to be like, this journey he spoke of with such authority? She didn't want to travel anywhere, alone with him. Suddenly the plane, with all its cargo of carnage, seemed a place of refuge.

She tried another tack. 'They say people in this situation should stay where they are. That they shouldn't go wandering off. That they should stay put.'

'In a lot of cases that's true, if

there's a chance of the wreck being spotted, but not here.' He was speaking quietly, steadily, as if holding back his impatience. 'D'you know there are five hundred planes from the last war, still lost somewhere in these jungles? And have you any idea how long it would take anyone to reach us, even if they knew where we were? No plane could land here. No helicopter could drop anyone. We'd be dead of hunger before they arrived.' His smile was grim. 'You can wait here if you want to. Me, I'm going.'

He picked up his jacket, and moved away from her, a decisive figure, broad of shoulder and narrow of hip, with a kind of fierce rough grace about him. He pushed through the leaves, and then she saw him sink out of sight, until finally his dark head disappeared through the plane's torn side. She could hear him moving, branches crackling. The sound seemed to be getting further away.

'Wait!' she screamed. 'Don't leave me!'

She scrambled after him, and when she reached the opening and looked down he was still standing there below her, an infuriating look on his face that told her he had known all along that she would follow.

'Have you got the bag?' he asked.

Kate clenched her teeth. 'Here's your damned bag,' she hissed, and flung it straight at him.

He fielded it easily, and dropped it on the ground beside him. 'Temper, temper!' Then he held out his arms. 'Come on. Jump down. It's quite easy.'

There was nothing else for it, she had to do as he said. Crouching in the opening she gathered her courage, and then launched herself forward.

He caught her as easily as he had the bag, and with as little ceremony, grabbing her by whatever portion of her anatomy came to hand. At least the jacket he had made her wear was loose enough to keep his touch impersonal.

Even so, she was clamped against him far too closely for her own comfort, his arms imprisoning her. She glanced up, and caught her breath. A shaft of sunlight catching him in its beam lit up his features. She had dismissed him as not being handsome, and perhaps he was not by any classical standard, but he was attractive. There was no doubt about that, he was devilishly and disturbingly attractive.

'Are you all right?'

'Of course I am,' she snapped. 'Let go. There's no need to suffocate me.'

His arms dropped away. 'I'll say this for you,' he drawled. 'You sure know how to thank a man.'

Kate regained her breath, and straightened her clothing. 'I wasn't aware that I had anything to be grateful about, Mr . . . er?'

'Oh, pardon me.' He made a little bow. 'I guess I thought the circumstances hardly called for etiquette. I should have introduced myself!'

Kate stared at him, chin up, her

blue eyes sparking angrily. 'Very funny . . . of course, if you'd rather I called you 'Hey You' for the rest of this trip . . . '

He laughed then. It was rather a grim laugh, but it was a good effort, thought Kate. Truth to tell, they neither of them had much to laugh about. She supposed that was why they were sniping at one another, it was a way of releasing the tension that lay just below the surface, a way of pretending everything was normal and under control, when actually nothing was under control, least of all her own emotions.

When he smiled she found it creased his brown face, making his eyes warmer, more gentle. 'I'm Matthew Selby, and everyone calls me Matt.'

She acknowledged it gravely. 'And I'm Katherine Summers. You can call me Kate, everyone does.'

Truce had been declared. It was an uneasy truce, as far as she was concerned, but she had no choice. Her very survival depended on this man; she knew that, but it was a hard pill to swallow. For years now she had made herself independent, free to live her own life, do her own thing, without a man having any real claim on her. That was how she had wanted it, and in the civilized world it had been easy enough, she had been able to make the terms, call the tune. But here it was very different, her instinct told her that Matt Selby was a very different proposition from easy-going Evan.

Matt Selby . . . the name rang a bell, in the same way that his face had seemed familiar, but she couldn't place it. She knew she had never met him before, he wasn't a man one would forget. She shrugged, and turned to look at her surroundings.

It was like being drowned in green; deep, lush green, a wild profusion of dense vegetation. Way, way above her was the canopy of the forest. She had to tilt her head back, to see where the trees soared towards the sky, letting in the sun in narrow brilliant beams in which danced a myriad of insects. The forest floor was springy; treacherous, rotting branches beneath the fallen leaves ready to give way beneath her feet. And just above her was the plane she had just left, hanging there.

'My God!' she whispered.

He put a hand on her shoulder, and for once it did not occur to her to jerk away.

'We were lucky to come out of it alive.' She nodded, unable to speak. 'We're not out of trouble yet,' he warned. 'It won't be easy.' He shouldered a rucksack he had acquired from somewhere, and picked up her bag. 'You may not be my ideal choice of a travelling companion in these circumstances, but I guess I'll have to get you out of this. *If* you do as I tell you, and *if* you can use a bit of common sense, we might just make it. Come along, Kate, like it or not you're going to have to come with me. We're on our own now.'

3

It seemed as if she had been climbing for hours. Kate knew it couldn't be so, because it was still light enough to see where they were putting their feet, though the brilliant shafts of sunlight had faded, draining the colour from trees and bushes. Resentfully obeying Matt Selby's instructions, she struggled behind him, her blue bag bumping uncomfortably against her back where he had tied it. She stepped carefully where he stepped, moving when he moved, pushing through dense jungle malevolently alive with creeping vines that tripped, thorns that clung and tore, and clouds of tiny black insects that rose from the bushes as they pushed their way through them. She was glad now that Matt had insisted on her wearing the long sleeved jacket, even though it was sticking to her, soaked with her own perspiration and with the water that dripped from the branches coating everything with a sheen of moisture.

She knew he must be feeling it too. His immaculate khaki trousers were already torn, and his jacket was as black with sweat as her own. All the same his lithe body moved inexorably ahead of her, clearing the way by brute strength, slashing at the creepers with his bare hands and a knife that was totally inadequate for the job. Not that that stopped him. He just kept going, an irresistible force.

Once or twice she had stopped, clinging to the trunk of a tree in weariness, but he just pressed on so that she had to catch up with him, cursing, until that broad back was once more within touching distance. Not that she wanted to touch him, she thought bitterly.

But although seemingly ignoring her, whenever they had to scale a particularly steep piece of rock, or wriggle through a dense bit of undergrowth, he turned to offer a hand. So far she had brushed aside his assistance, but now she had come to the end of her strength.

'Mr. Selby . . . Matt . . . I can't go on.'

He kept on climbing, and she screamed, hating him. 'Did you hear me? I can't go on any more.'

He slithered back down to her. She expected him to be scathing. He had made it quite clear that her presence there was a complication. She tensed herself to meet his attack, but he only held out his hand.

'Give me your bag.'

He undid the knots that fastened it, and slung it over his shoulder, where it bounced against the knapsack he was already carrying. 'Come on.'

Kate sank down onto a wet, moss-covered log. She leaned wearily back against a tangle of branches and closed her eyes. 'I can't.'

He didn't answer, and she sat there,

taking deep gulping breaths, trying to shift the stitch that had been threatening her side for some time. Would he go on and leave her there to die? She hardly cared if he did. At last, though, the stitch eased and the silence became oppressive, seeping through her consciousness until her curiosity got the better of her, and she opened her eyes. He was crouching opposite her, waiting impassively, his dark eyes fixed on her face. His very immobility irked her. He was like a great wild animal crouching there, so still, watching her. She shivered, and roused herself.

'Why did we have to start now, anyway?' She was aware of sounding petulant, but couldn't help herself. He was too overpowering, too sublimely confident. Didn't he ever discuss things, ask someone else's opinion? What gave him the right to be so almighty sure that they were doing the correct thing? 'Why couldn't we have waited until the morning, when we were fresh?'

Something that was just less than a smile passed over his face. 'D'you really think you'd have felt any better after a night in that plane?' he asked. 'Things would have become . . .' he hesitated, as though searching for a delicate way of putting it, 'unpleasant there, shortly.'

Kate became aware of the heat and the background buzzing of insects, and knew with a shudder what he meant.

'Besides which,' he added, 'we don't have much food, so every hour counts. We have to press on while we still have the strength.' He rose to his feet. 'Just a few minutes more, and then we'll stop for the night. I promise. Just a little further.' He moved off, taking it for granted that she would follow.

'Wait a minute,' said Kate, and when he turned, frowning with impatience, added quietly. 'Give me back the bag. You need your hands free.'

They started again, slipping on wet roots, grabbing at branches that broke even as they pulled on them, all the time climbing. Kate had no idea where they were heading; she doubted if he knew himself. There was no proper trail, nothing to show that human feet had ever trod such a wilderness, but she followed him all the same. His very confidence was comforting.

At last he stopped where the trees opened out onto a wider ledge. 'OK. This'll do.'

Kate heaved a sigh of relief, and flopped onto a clear piece of ground. Matt tossed his knapsack down beside her, and shrugged off his jacket. Then he began tearing at the trees, breaking off branches. She watched him with curiosity, unwillingly admiring his lean hard-muscled body.

'What are you doing?'

He dragged the branches across to where there were two fallen trees, and laid them across the trunks until he had created a rough platform. 'You are a one for asking questions! I'm making our bed. Unless you want to sleep in the mud, or intend to sit up all night.'

She swallowed, a coil of unease snaking through her. She hadn't thought about how they would sleep, or wash, or eat, or any of the intimate things she would have to perform while in this stranger's company. It was becoming increasingly obvious to her, though, that this was no time to be fastidious. She shifted uneasily, fighting her own reluctance, until in the end she simply had to speak.

'I . . . er . . . I have to go behind that bush,' she said stiffly. 'I'm telling you so that you can . . . '

'Respect your privacy?' He gave an unexpected chuckle, looking at her sideways, grinning. He broke another branch. 'Go ahead Kate, but watch where you go. Some spiders around here can bite.'

She gave him a dubious look. Perhaps he had been teasing her, she didn't know. She wouldn't put it past him, but on the other hand it was quite likely that there were all kinds of creeping, crawling insects amongst the

58

leaves. She withdrew behind a bush, inspecting every twig with suspicion. She had always had a horror of such things, indeed her dread of them was so strong that she was even grateful for the fact that a man was crashing about, only a few feet away from her.

No spiders came crawling out to meet her, and at last with a sigh of relief, her needs attended to, she began to pull up the denim trousers. Then her eyes dilated with horror. On the soft white flesh of one thigh hung something black and swollen. Feverishly she pushed her trousers lower to investigate, and lower still; then screaming she stumbled and tore her way back to Matt, her trousers abandoned.

Alarmed, he leaped to meet her, a stick in his hand. 'What the hell? What's the matter?'

Stammering, Kate flung herself at him. 'Look . . . oh, loo . . . look. Get them off me. Quick . . . ' Shuddering, she began pulling at the obscenities.

'Don't do that!' He grabbed at her

hands, restraining her. 'They're only leeches, Kate. They won't really hurt.'

'Get them off me!' she shrieked, shaking one long leg after the other.

'Keep still.' He rummaged in her bag, bringing out the matches. 'Don't pull them off, or the wounds won't heal. You have to make them let go.'

'Hurry. Oh, please hurry!'

One by one he struck a match and applied the flame, and the leeches dropped from her like fly-blown grapes, leaving strings of blood across her skin. She shivered as if she had a fever, her teeth chattering. 'Are they all gone?'

He turned her round, his hands gentle. 'The lower half's clear. What about the top, under your blouse?'

With a little scream Kate tore off her jacket and blouse, thrusting them into his hands, oblivious to anything but the disgusting slug-like creatures. 'Are there any on my back?' she demanded. 'Quick . . . tell me. Are there any more there?'

His hands brushed across her shoulder

bones, and down her ribs. 'No . . . oo,' he murmured doubtfully. 'Turn round.'

She whirled around obediently, eyes huge and beseeching in a face grown pale. 'Can you see any?'

'No . . . oo.' She couldn't understand the quirk of his lips, the laughter in his eyes. Then she suddenly awoke to her situation. God, what was she thinking of? No wonder he was laughing, eyeing her, and obviously not too tired to be thoroughly enjoying it.

With a strangled cry of protest she snatched her silk top from him and struggled back into it, grimacing as its clammy dampness settled on her skin, and turned away from him, cringing with embarrassment, to find her trousers.

'Hang on, we've got to clean those wounds.'

Without even waiting for her to answer he rummaged about in her bag until he came across the cleaning tissues. 'These'll do.'

He unscrewed the brandy flask.

'Shame to waste this, but I'm hoping it'll kill any germs. It's not the leeches you have to worry about, it's infection in this climate.'

He knelt in front of her, dabbing at the stinging, reddened marks on her legs, one hand firmly clasped around her thigh, his dark head bowed below her, his neck bent. It was a strong brown neck, set on powerfully wide shoulders. His unruly hair was too long, it curled at the nape, sticking to skin that glistened with the sheen of sweat.

She swallowed painfully, her throat suddenly dry. She wanted to move, to run, to do anything to break the spell. This couldn't be her, feeling such strange and unwanted sensations. She was appalled, but she stood rooted to the spot, and slowly her hand crept forward to touch his head.

'There, that should do it.'

He looked up, and his eyes caught her own. He knew. To her utter mortification, she could see that he had recognized the fascination that had made her lips soften and part. To her shame she saw that he knew it. He was the kind of man who would always know.

It had been there since the first time he had looked at her at the airport. Something inside her had rung alarm bells. Told her to run. Warned her that here was a man who might have the power to awaken the very thing in her that she had been stifling these past years.

She jerked away from him. 'Thank you,' she croaked. 'I'm sorry I panicked. I'll get dressed now.'

'No you won't . . . not yet, at any rate.' She saw to her horror that Matt Selby was stripping the shirt from his brown muscular back, undoing his belt, dropping his trousers, hopping on one leg as he pulled them off.

Her heart leaped into her mouth. 'What . . . are you doing?' she gasped breathlessly.

'D'you think you have a monopoly

on leeches?' he grunted. 'Here . . . get the damned things off me now.'

The breath left her lungs in a rush of relief, and embarrassment at her own thoughts. Gritting her teeth, she did as he asked. There were a couple of leeches on his back, they must have dropped down from the branches and worked their way under his shirt. Her fingers trembling she applied the flame, afraid of burning the bronzed skin of his shoulders. He turned around, but there were none in the wiry black hair that matted his chest and descended in a vee to the flat muscles of his stomach. As with herself most of the leeches had attached themselves to his legs.

Each time she applied the flame to a black body she had to brush it off with her fingers, and in her still heightened state of awareness she did not know which disturbed her the most, the swollen leeches, or the unfamiliar feel of his muscular legs under her hands. They were strong legs, sturdy with hard thighs and dark hair clinging damply to

64

them. She stroked them clean, thinking with surprise that she had never studied a man's legs before; it was intriguing the way the hair lay in tight whorls against his skin . . .

'Er . . . if that's the lot I'll look elsewhere myself, if you don't mind.'

She looked up him, startled, to see him grinning down at her. She gulped, the blood rising hot into her face. 'I don't think there are any more. I'll . . . I'll go and find my trousers.'

She fled, hiding behind the bushes, panic ripping through her. Out of his sight, she stopped, standing with shaking hands pressed against blazing cheeks. It was her own feelings that had shocked her. She should have agreed to marry Evan, and made herself safe. Men like Matt Selby were dangerous!

'Are you all right, Kate?'

'Yes,' she answered quickly. 'I'm coming.' She forced herself to dress and walk back to him, stiff with apprehension, wondering how she was going to meet his eyes. When she reached him, though, he was was busy covering the platform of branches with a thick layer of broad green pandanus leaves, and he didn't bother looking at her at all.

'Not bad,' he said. 'Now how about my dinner?'

She cast him a wary glance. He was as at home as if he was lounging on a sofa in the parlour. He patted the space beside him. 'Let's see what we've got before it gets too dark to notice what we're eating.'

Relieved to find him so matter-of-fact, she relaxed and joined him. Thankful to be doing something completely harmless and unable to be misconstrued, she rummaged into the bags and brought out what they had. 'Ham sandwiches, sir,' she said with a half-hearted attempt at a laugh, 'or cheese and pickle, and a half an apple.'

He gave the matter considerable thought. 'We'll have half of the ham ones each, Kate, because they won't keep, and the apple. The cheese should still be edible tomorrow.'

She fell silent, sitting beside him, handing him half of the curling sandwiches. The sudden grimness of his expression brought home to her that this was no game, no picnic. How long would it take them to reach safety, if they ever did? Instinctively she knew that if anyone could bring them safely back to civilization, this man could, and in spite of the fact he obviously found her a nuisance, and that she found him unsettling, she was glad he was there.

Dusk fell quickly, almost without them noticing. The air was cooler, the shadows darkening, the night alive with the sound of living things, crickets and cicadas making a constant background whirring, punctuated by another shrill sound.

'Tree frogs,' Matt said laconically. 'They come out now to feed on insects.' He looked thoughtful. 'I suppose they would make a meal for us.'

'You're joking!' said Kate.

'I've never been more serious. Don't worry though, we haven't quite come to that yet. I'll see if I can't catch something tomorrow, though it's no use until we can light a fire, and it's too wet here. When we get higher it will be better. Night is the time to hunt, everything comes out then. The bats are out too.'

'Bats!' She instinctively moved a little closer to him.

He chuckled. 'They won't get in your hair, Kate. Not even in that glorious mop of yours.'

He thought her hair glorious! An uncalled-for feeling of pleasure stabbed through her. Though goodness knows it didn't really matter what he thought about her looks. And her hair didn't feel very glorious now, dishevelled, tangled and full of dead leaves.

She chewed pensively on the dried crust of her sandwich. 'You seem to know an awful lot about this jungle.'

'So I should. It's my job.'

She waited. A companionable atmosphere had crept up on them, a delicate thing, like a flower starting to open. It could easily be damaged. She was afraid to force anything. He was, she thought with a sudden flash of insight, a very private man.

'Nature Conservation,' he said after a while. 'Checking the forests. I've been working here on and off for years. These are some of the few rain forests left in the world.'

A memory stirred in Kate . . . something she had seen or read. She let him continue, as he warmed to his subject.

'Man is fast destroying his most precious commodity, the trees. When they're gone the weather will change . . . then there'll be more soil erosion, drought, starvation . . .'

'Now I know who you are!' she interrupted, pleased with herself. 'Of course, no wonder I recognised you . . .'

She regretted speaking. He clammed up, shrugging. 'I guess I do get publicity.'

That was putting it mildly. Trouble-shooter for the World Conservation Congress, the press never stopped featuring his photograph on the front page, usually allied to controversial headlines. Not that anyone objected to conservation. Most people paid it lip-service, but he did more than that. Said to be a wealthy man in his own right, he had thrown himself into the cause, heart and soul.

'You can hardly expect to avoid publicity,' she remarked, 'if you go about things the way you do. Wasn't there something about breaking a man's nose because he'd chopped down some old trees? Are you always violent?'

It was too dark to see his expression, but she could hear the smile in his voice. 'Only if I don't get what I want.'

The way he said it sent a shudder through her, and he noticed it. 'It's getting chilly. Here, I brought these.'

She'd wondered what he had packed in his knapsack. Now she knew. Two cellular blankets that had been part of the plane's equipment. He spread them out. 'Snuggle down, Kate. They'll probably be wet by morning, but at least they're dry now.'

She lay back, and he tucked one of the blankets around her, right up to her chin. The pandanus leaves were thick and springy, making a comfortable mattress. For the first time since meeting him she felt secure. She returned to her thoughts about the man at her side. What else had she read about him? Ah yes, she had it now . . . he was part North American Indian. That accounted for his looks, and also, if she remembered rightly, he had been adopted by a rich industrialist who had died leaving him a fortune.

She grimaced, thinking that it was no wonder she had reacted so violently to his masculinity. So, presumably, had those women who were shadowy figures in the background of the press photographs. Perhaps it said something about Matt Selby's charisma, that it was only *his* face she remembered.

It was dark now, and she lay staring into the blackness, listening to the sounds of the night, the rustlings and cracklings, and slitherings. She wondered if there were snakes. She asked him.

'Sure, several,' he answered. 'Pythons, for instance. They hunt at night too.'

'Thank you *very* much.'

'Well, you asked me.'

Would they ever reach Wiatapi? she wondered. And if they didn't, would there be anyone to miss her? Certainly not Evan, she thought. Oh, he would be shocked and upset, but it would soon heal. He would miss her for a while, and then he would find himself a nice girl who would give him the affection he deserved. And her mother — oh, she did hope her mother would miss her, a little bit. If she didn't, she had only herself to blame.

What a mess she had made of her life. What good was fame and financial reward, when there was nobody to whom she really mattered?

'Matt,' she said softly.

'Mmm?'

'If . . . if you don't make it, is there anyone at home who will be terribly upset?'

She felt him turn to her in the darkness. 'What makes you ask that?'

'I don't know,' she said softly. 'I was just thinking . . . I don't believe anybody would weep many tears over me.'

'I find that hard to believe.' His voice sounded warm and lazy beside her ear. He paused for a moment. 'I've made my share of enemies, but, yes, there are people who would care.'

Kate thought of all the women in the photographs. 'I can imagine,' she said drily. 'There must be at least a dozen hearts ready to break, if you haven't broken them already.'

She felt him rise on his elbow, as if he was trying to see her face through the heavy, scented darkness of the night. 'I do like the opposite sex,' he said, and his voice purred deeply like that of a big cat. 'There's nothing wrong in that. Don't you, Kate?'

A warning tingle spread up her spine. This was a silly conversation. She didn't like the way it was going.

'You don't, do you?' he persisted. 'You don't like men at all. Or is it only me?'

Before she could answer, he reached out to her face, his fingers warm against her skin as he traced the contours of her cheeks. She couldn't bear it . . . this sensation of careering out of control every time he touched her. She was going to have to stop it, once and for all.

She pushed his hand away. 'Let's get one thing clear, Mr. Selby,' she said coldly. 'I may have to travel with you, but that's all. You're quite right, I don't like you. And I'd rather you kept your hands to yourself.'

His hand withdrew, only to be placed on the leaves at the far side of her head, so that he was leaning over her. She stiffened defensively, feeling his breath on her face, the warmth of his body as he loomed, a darker mass against the blackness that surrounded them. 'Is that so?' he murmured, and there was a note in his voice that boded no good. 'Well, I might just take notice of that, Kate — if I believed you.'

'No!' Instinctively she knew what was coming next, and twisted her head away from him. Any minute now his mouth would find hers. Her imagination ran riot. Even thinking about it, everything seemed to slow down, her limbs growing langourous and warm.

She gritted her teeth. He could have his kiss; it would prove nothing, except that she was telling the truth. She would be like a stone. *That* was what she felt about him . . . but she knew she was lying to herself. She didn't know how to handle this, she had always been in control of her emotions, for . . . oh, these many years.

Time seemed to hang between them.

They were joined by it, welded together, so near and yet still not touching. She could hear her own telltale breathing speeding up. She tried to hold her breath, expecting his mouth to swoop at any moment. And then, just when she felt she could not bear it any longer, he rolled away from her. 'Point made, I think,' he said a trifle smugly.

The shock left her speechless for a second. Then, 'How dare you!' she stormed. 'If you were at all civilized . . .'

'But I'm not,' he said briefly. 'I'm half Sioux.' He tucked the blankets closer, ignoring her involuntary movement of alarm, and then leaned nearer her again, his voice low and vehement.

'Just now I need trouble from you, Kate, like I need a hole in the head. You don't have to be frightened of me. I'll not touch you again, unless you ask me to, but I'll tell you this. You wanted me to kiss you! I don't know why you're lying, Kate, but your body was telling the truth. I can't stand people who lie, Kate. Remember that.'

He turned his back on her, and she lay staring into nothingness, hot tears of shame welling up in her eyes and trickling down her cheeks. She turned her head to one side and angrily brushed the tears away, lying rigid, not wanting him to know that she was crying, not wanting even to admit to herself that what he had said was true.

She *had* wanted him to kiss her.

4

'Come on, time to get moving.'

Kate opened her eyes and looked up into the canopy of leaves. It was early morning, and the light filtering through was cool and speckly green, like an underwater grotto. Matt Selby, stripped to the waist, was washing with a handkerchief soaked in water caught in the hollow of a tree trunk. Kate watched, fascinated in spite of herself by the play of muscles in his lean, powerful back. He turned, and she could see the sheen of damp skin, the dark hair plastered wetly on his chest.

'Have you, er . . . seen enough?'

Kate snapped back to the fact that she had been staring at him with open appreciation, and he was grinning back at her, his eyes challenging, daring her to remember the episode of the previous night.

'More than enough,' she said drily, angry with herself for revealing anything of her inner turmoil. Pushing back her blanket she struggled to her feet. She felt stiff and aching, and under that was a dull gnawing feeling that reminded her she had not eaten anything substantial since lunch-time of the day before. She sighed, and folded the blanket, stuffing it away in Matt's knapsack.

'Have a wash,' said Matt. 'It'll make you feel better.' He handed her the handkerchief. 'You can dry off with this other one. It's the best I can offer you . . . unless you'd like to strip off, and I'll shake a few branches to provide you with a shower?'

Her startled glance told her he was joking. She ventured a small smile. 'I don't think so, if you don't mind.'

'Spoil-sport!'

He disappeared from view amongst the under-growth. For a moment she waited, then understanding that he was giving her the opportunity of some privacy, she did the best she could to freshen up. She felt all the better for it, the water was full of small insects and bits of leaves, but it was cool and refreshing. It made it almost unbearable to have to dress again in clothes by now stained and grubby. Oh, what she wouldn't give for a bath! But it was her hair she despaired of. Cursing herself for her stupidity in leaving her comb behind with her makeup, she raked through it with her fingers. In desperation she broke off a small piece of pliant vine, and managed to tie it back.

Then there was nothing else to do but sit down to wait for Matt, hunching up her knees, wrapping her arms around them. The dappled light that fell across her face threw shadows across it, accentuating its fine lines, the anxiety in eyes turned to dark violet. She turned sharply at every tiny sound. It was surprising how noisy the forest was. Birds, she supposed, listening to the raucous shrieks and chatterings that echoed through the trees. A flash of red and blue parrots confirmed this. Kate strained her ears for any sign of Matt's return — but there was nothing.

He'll be back soon, she told herself hopefully. Last night she had wished him anywhere . . . the further away the better. She had wanted to die rather than face him again, and yet here she was on edge because he was out of sight. And it wasn't just because she was frightened of the jungle, she was honest enough with herself to admit that.

Why, she wondered painfully, had last night had such a devastating effect on her? She had kissed men before, Evan included, but it had never had the effect of the kiss that had never arrived. Always she had been the one conferring a favour. She had been able to hold back, had been in control of the situation and of her own feelings, but last night a deeper and more primitive part of herself had taken over. It had been only a moment, a split second of awareness for both of them. Yes, it *had* been for both of them, for all that he pretended he had been teaching her a lesson. It wasn't surprising really, after what they had been through — the crash, the horror of finding themselves the only survivors, the hard trek through the forest. They had both been on edge, their perceptions heightened, the adrenalin flowing. It meant nothing. She was sophisticated enough to know that. And *he* wouldn't be worrying himself about it, she felt sure of that.

But then, Matt Selby was a man who was used to having his own way. It would only have been a game to him ... and she had no intention of becoming one of the players. Because she didn't play games. She didn't like the rules!

Where was he? She began to grow uneasy, listening to the alien sounds of the forest that seemed to close in around her. Perhaps she was wrong. Perhaps he was fed up with her; she was just a burden, something that would impede his progress and slow him up. Without her, he would no doubt move twice as quickly. Perhaps he had abandoned her. In sudden panic she looked around her, and relaxed as she found the bag with the food in it. He would never leave without that, surely. She poked into the bag and looked longingly at the unappetising remains of the sandwiches. Better not to eat them yet. There would be time enough when Matt came back, if he came back . . .

'Hi there . . . waiting for breakfast?'

She spun around with relief, her eyes lighting up with a welcome she could not hide.

'I . . . didn't hear you come,' she faltered, feeling as though her breath had suddenly been squeezed out of her.

He gave her a mocking look. 'I told you I was half Sioux.' He picked up the bag of food. 'Here, we'd better finish off these sandwiches while they're still edible. If you're very good I'll let you have a biscuit.'

'I can hardly wait!'

He brought her water cupped in a leaf. He kept well out of her reach, making it obvious that he wasn't about to risk touching her, even by accident. She had the bewildering thought that it would have been comforting, if he had put his arms around her — just once.

They ate slowly, savouring every morsel, making it last, his eyes on her face all the time.

'How did you manage to creep up on me without my hearing?' she asked at last, simply for the sake of something to say.

'Creep up, Kate?' His eyebrows shot up. 'What d'you think I am, a peeping Tom? I've better things to do than spy on you.' He rose to his feet as if he had tired of the whole subject. 'Come on, then. Time we were going.'

Kate picked up her bag, dissatisfied, as though something between them had been left unsaid. She hoisted it onto her back, and it slid off. She tried it again, and balanced it this time, but when she tried to tie the liana thongs it slipped once more. Matt just stood looking on, a lop-sided grin on his face. He looked like a disreputable brigand, she decided angrily, with a day's dark stubble of beard and his hair wilder than ever.

'A gentleman would help,' she said icily.

'But I might have to touch you . . . and that's not allowed.'

She stiffened. 'Will you stop smirking and fix it?'

'Are you asking?' he drawled.

She flashed him a look of frustrated fury. 'Oh, very well! I'm asking. Satisfied?'

He had it fixed in no time, easing it high on her shoulders so that she could take the weight without tiring, crossing the vines in front of her and tying them at her waist. He stood very close while he fastened them, his knuckles brushing her breast. Kate shivered as she felt the now familiar hot tendrils of excitement

85

that his touch brought. He noticed her shiver, and his lips tightened. 'Don't get the wrong idea,' he said curtly. 'I'm not trying anything.' And he turned away to pick up his own knapsack.

She should have felt relieved, perhaps it was safer that way. What did it matter what he felt about her, anyway? If they got out of here they would go their separate ways, and she would forget all about him.

They started climbing once more, and Kate had no more time to worry about his reactions, or even her own. The day wore on in an exhausted haze of putting one foot in front of another, avoiding branches that snapped back in her face, disentangling herself from thorns. Matt set such a cracking pace that she found it hard to keep up, and started lagging behind so that he had to stop patiently on occasions, to let her catch up. At length they came to a part where the ground turned to steep slippery rocks, and then he made her take the lead.

'That's to keep you moving,' he explained. 'We've got to make better time, and if you don't keep going you'll get a smack on that pretty little backside of yours.'

'You . . . ' She whirled around angrily. 'Don't you lay a finger on me. You promised.'

He looked unrepentant. 'Promises are like piecrusts, Kate. Meant to be broken. It's up to you. Go fast enough, and you'll be quite safe.'

The threat was enough. She scrambled ahead of him, slipping and sliding on the treacherous surface. Once she lost her footing completely, and fell backwards into his arms. He broke her fall, and set her gently on her feet again in an almost impersonal manner. In spite of what he had said he was keeping to his word. It probably wasn't too difficult for him, she decided. She wasn't likely to attract any man, looking the way she did . . . dirty and dishevelled and completely lacking in sex appeal. And that was good, because she didn't want to attract Matt Selby.

She shivered suddenly, wondering in spite of herself what it would be like if he did break his word, while she was so completely at his mercy. The thought of those strong arms holding her did nothing for her composure.

'Where are we going?' she asked wearily in one of the rare moments when he allowed her to rest.

'Over this crest.' He pointed up ahead. 'From the top we'll be able to see the rivers and I'll know where we are. It's not so steep that side. There's better hunting there, and that's why there are villages. We'll meet up with one of the tribes sooner or later.'

It was hard to believe anyone could live in such an inhospitable place. She remembered reading somewhere that there had been headhunters well within living memory, and that there were still places where it was not safe to venture. She had looked forward to exploring with a proper guide from the lodge at Wiatapi, but here . . .

'What are the natives like?'

'Friendly, I hope.' He sounded amused. 'Don't worry Kate. They're quite safe. I've lived amongst them.' He rolled up his sleeve, and she could see a livid line of scars down his upper arm. 'See that? I was awarded that at a cutting ceremony. It's the crocodile mark . . . made me one of the people. Fella-belong-Trees. That's me.'

What a man this was! Was there anything he had not done? she wondered wryly as they pressed on. She contrasted him mentally with all the other men she had ever known, and they faded into insignificance. How would Evan shape up against him? Poor Evan . . . there was no comparison. And what would she do about Evan, if she ever made it back? Well, she knew the answer to that. That much she had learned about herself. She could never marry Evan, it would not be fair.

'This is a good place to stop, Kate.

If you want to. We can have a biscuit and a rest.'

She had been climbing so blindly that she had hardly noticed that they had arrived at a small clearing; a level place where the sun shone through drying up the ground.

'The trees aren't quite so thick here,' she panted as she wriggled out of her pack. 'It was like walking through a tunnel back there, the light hardly penetrated at all.'

'We can't be far from the top now,' he told her. 'The vegetation will be sparse there. It gets cold at nights, freezing sometimes.'

'Oh good,' she moaned, collapsing wearily into a heap. 'We've been stewed by the heat, soaked with drizzling rain, eaten by leeches . . . to be frozen will be quite a change.'

'Look upon it as an experience,' he chuckled as he divided out the biscuits. 'You're lucky to be treading where no white woman has ever been before. Isn't it beautiful!'

She looked at him in amazement. Beautiful! He must be out of his mind. But there was an expression of rapt pleasure on his strong features. He really meant it!

She looked about her, trying to see it with his eyes, and nodded slowly. She had been too afraid, too exhausted, to notice it before, but there *was* beauty here. Peperonia creepers entwined the soaring trunks of the mengaris trees, chains of bright red flowers swung above their heads, and sudden showers of orange butterflies rose from the bushes. Birds called around them. As Kate's eyes became accustomed to searching the gloom between the trees she began to see flashes of colour, rusty reds, greens, blues, orange.

'What are they?'

'Rainbow bee-eaters. There are birds of paradise, too.' He pointed out other things that had been hidden to her before, giant hover flies, a snake-eyed skink scuttling into the undergrowth, a giant millipede.

He was enthusiastic, using the odd telling turn of phrase, a description, that revealed his love for all the creatures of nature. She looked at the lithe figure beside her with more respect. He had the soul of an artist. The unexpected revelation surprised and pleased her. She found she wanted to know more about him. Wanted it with surprising force. If they didn't get out of here, he would be the last person she ever came to know . . . and although it wouldn't matter then, she wanted to know him properly, not just the veneer that anyone might see.

'Where were you brought up?' she asked with genuine interest. 'Your adopted father was Thomas Selby, wasn't he? The industrialist?'

His face creased in a smile, lighting up his eyes, little creases of humour at their corners. 'Yes . . . he found me in a reserve when he was passing through one day. I was only a nipper. My father had been a passing Gringo . . . my mother was weighed down with kids, and sickly. He took a shine to me, goodness knows why. He said it was because I sassed him back. Nobody ever talked back to Thomas Selby.'

Kate's lips twitched. He had obviously learned much from the man who befriended him. 'But you didn't want to carry on his business, his empire?' So many men would have done, would have given anything to be in his shoes, rich enough and powerful enough to indulge their every whim. But not him. She had known that, even before she asked him.

He shook his head. 'I couldn't stand being shut in an office. He knew that, and he knew I never forgot my early days. I guess he cared about me enough not to want to change me. He taught me that if I wanted to help my people I had to become influential. It took time, but I learned. And . . .' his voice tailed away.

'Go on,' urged Kate. 'Please!'

He looked surprised, but continued. 'I learned it wasn't just the North

93

American Indians that needed protection, but the land they lived on. And not just their land, either.'

He idly picked up a twig, and broke it between his fingers. 'My maternal grandfather used to take me camping.' He looked up at her briefly, with a wry smile. 'Most of the young braves have lost the old ways and skills you know, but he insisted on teaching me.' His voice grew quiet. 'He could move through a forest and not even a sitting bird would hear him coming. He was a great man.' He seemed miles away from her, lost in a dream.

'But your adopted father, he was great too?'

He came back from whatever past memories he had been immersed in, and laughed fondly. 'Oh yes, he taught me a lot. Different things, though.' He turned to her, his head on one side, looking at her thoughtfully, and his eyes were unfathomable. 'What is it about you, Kate, that makes me babble on about myself? It's not usually my

94

way. Anyway, what about you? Bound for a holiday at Wiatapi?'

A holiday! Was that what he thought her, one of those rich social butterflies with nothing on her mind but an endless round of pleasure?

'I can't waste time on expensive holidays,' she told him succinctly. 'I have to work for my living. I write and illustrate books — about myths, folklore mainly. I've just finished one about . . . '

'The land of The Waugal. I know. I saw your exhibition.'

'You did!' She wasn't quite as surprised as she would have been, only hours before. She was beginning to know something of the inner sensitivity of this man. But she still had a lot to learn about him, and she found herself willing to be a pupil.

'I liked your work,' he continued. 'It reminded me of my own people. In fact I bought something. The one inspired by cave paintings . . . '

'That was you!' A shaft of pleasure shot through her at the thought that he had liked something she had created, liked it enough to make it his own. 'I'm . . . glad,' she said softly. 'But how did you know who I was?'

He looked amused. 'I asked. At the plane. I looked at the flight list, with so few passengers it wasn't hard to work out which you were.' So it had not been quite a coincidence that he had sat beside her. The knowledge made her feel uneasy. Why had he taken the trouble? Was he just another man after an easy conquest?

'Isn't it time we moved on?' she said stiffly.

The rest of the day followed in much the same way as before, except that the trees were thinning out now, and she could see the sky. The biscuits did not sustain her for long, and she began to feel hollow inside, and slightly dizzy. Matt still made her lead the way, but she had begun to understand that it was for her own safety's sake that he did so, and not out of sheer bloody mindedness, as she had first thought. So many times he was there to catch her when she slipped, was ready to bind her feet when she began to blister, was insistent that she checked for the leeches that still plagued them, and disinfected the wounds with the remaining brandy. Sweat ran down her body in rivulets, and her strength seemed to ebb with it until she hardly had the energy to be bothered to wave away the swarms of small flies which irritated beyond belief.

There was only one thing she was thankful for — and even that was a mixed blessing — there was no shortage of water. Moisture coated everything they touched, condensing on leaves, and dripping from trees and rocks. Twice they found their way blocked by streams that cascaded down the precipitous slope. The air was still and dank. This was the high-altitude cloud forest, he told her, and they could not expect it to get any better until they broke out of it, free from the rain-clouds, to the top.

★ ★ ★

It was another day before that happened. Three days they had been travelling. It seemed like an eternity. Kate had come to rely on Matt completely. Whenever she was about to give up, he made her carry on. She had long since stopped worrying about what he thought of her, or how she felt about him. She would be glad to feel anything, she was so numb, and so hungry. They had finished the biscuits, and the wine gums. Matt caught a small lizard, but as he had predicted it was impossible to find any kindling dry enough to make a fire, and hungry as she was she could not bring herself to chew on its raw flesh. She wanted to, she was hungry enough for anything, but her stomach rebelled.

'You must try,' he insisted. She raised resentful hollow eyes, her hair

98

loose now, and dripping around her face. 'Oh . . . leave me alone,' she groaned. 'What does it matter to you what I do?'

'Enough to see that I get you back safely. Do as I say.'

Stifling a sob she chewed on a morsel he had hacked off with his knife, and gagged, but swallowed. 'I'll never complain if my steak's overdone again,' she vowed.

He humoured her. 'I fancy roast potatoes, all golden on the outside and fluffy inside.'

'Oh, don't. All I want is a square meal — anything will do, and a bath.'

'You shall have both,' he told her. 'Come on, Kate. Get moving . . . we've got to get over the ridge today.'

'You're a bully,' she declared, but her words lacked conviction. She knew he would not let her die, not if it was within his power. Why she had ever thought him like David she would never know, the two men were quite, quite different. Strangely enough, she could hardly remember David's face. He no longer haunted her dreams. She had a new devil on her back now: her days and nights revolved around a man who did nothing but torment her, even if it was for her own good.

Wearily she dragged herself to her feet, and he helped her. Where, she wondered, had the agreement about not touching disappeared to? It had vanished somewhere, along with her pride, and her independence. All that remained was the stubborn determination not to let Matt see that she cared. He had become important to her, too important, she realized. She depended on him for her safety, her comfort, her very life. And since that first night, he had not laid a finger on her, except to help. She wished he would. She desperately needed to rest in his arms. She needed the warmth of his body to ease her weariness. She needed the reassurance that somebody cared.

'Not far now,' he said. 'We'll be

over the top, and things will get better, you'll see.'

Recognizing that she was losing strength, he took the lead, half pulling her after him. The forest floor was treacherous here, the ground hollow, made up of fallen branches covered by leaves. They had been climbing for another hour when she slipped and fell. Her foot went right through the false surface, with a sickening, wrenching pain.

'Kate!' He was at her side, lifting her, holding her as she burst into sobs against his shoulder. Her leg was scraped from knee to ankle, the blood oozing out in tiny droplets. He cleaned it, and bound it up with one of the cleaner handkerchiefs, and gave her two pain killers.

'I'm sorry,' she sniffed. 'I'm not showing up very well, am I? It's just . . . I'm so tired. And hungry too.'

'You're doing fine,' he said 'We're nearly there, at the top of the ridge. You've got to keep going, Kate.'

'I can't . . . ' she wailed.

'You can. You have to.'

'No, leave me. I can't take any more.'

He exploded then, shaking her until her teeth rattled. 'You're useless,' he shouted. 'D'you know that?'

'Well then, go on without me,' she sobbed. 'I never asked you to take me with you, anyway.'

'Oh no?' The anger rose in his voice, and something else. He was turning into a complete stranger. His grip was tightening on her, hurting. 'There's only one thing you'd be good for, and if you're not going to make it, I might as well have that, here and now!'

She gasped, pulling away from him, her eyes wide as she realized what he meant. 'You . . . you don't mean that,' she stammered. 'I know you don't . . . I . . . '

'You know *nothing*!' His face was frighteningly unfamiliar, his eyes calculating. 'You're nothing but a little tease, Kate. D'you think I don't know?

You've wanted me, ever since we've met, but you've been dangling me on a hook. Well, the time for that is past. I have my needs too — did you never think of that?'

He undid the buttons of her jacket, flicking them open, one by one. Kate froze, her mind numbed by his change in attitude. With a sudden movement he slid the jacket off her shoulders. 'D'you want to scream?' he murmured, his voice strange. 'Go ahead . . . there's no one to hear.' His hands began stroking, setting her body on fire.

'No . . . ' gasped Kate. 'Oh please . . . Matt . . . no.'

He lowered his head, until his lips touched hers. They sent waves of electricity coursing through her. She had thought herself beyond any response, in her exhausted state, but she had been wrong. Sensations rose now, like snakes uncoiling from a sleep. They writhed through her body, taking over its movements, filling her with energy, making her want him with such fierce

103

abandon that her hands of their own accord began to cling and caress.

And yet this was not what she wanted! Oh God, no. The realization came to her in a blinding flash. She wanted him, yes, but not mindlessly, carelessly like this. She wanted him . . . with love!

Ah, so that was the pain that seared through her. She knew it at last. She loved him. It had happened slowly, against her will, so slowly that she had not understood. She had come to love the man she thought she knew . . . the man with the soul of an artist, the man who cared for his people and his land, who had cared for and protected her. But she had been wrong. It had all been a sham.

'No!' she cried hoarsely. 'Stop . . . please. Let's go now. Please Matt, I mean it. I can do it. Let me go while I still have strength to travel.'

He raised his head. His eyes burned into hers, and she had a crazy urge to reach up and touch his face, his rough, tough face with the black hair hanging over his eyes, the shadow of a wiry beard now beginning to cover the strong jaw. But she stayed absolutely still.

He sighed. Then he moved away from her, and tugged her clothes straight. He tossed her the jacket. 'Come on then, girl. We've wasted enough time.'

She found, when she rose to her feet, that the blood was coursing through her veins faster than ever before. Anger fired her steps, and she kept pace with him without speaking, until they broke out of the forest and found themselves at the top of the world.

The sky was clear, the air crisp dry and cold . . . cold enough to make her shiver. At first they walked through rhododendrons, glowing red and orange, then even this changed to bare outcrops of black rock, and grass spangled with daisies and buttercups. Below them, on the far side of the peak, green and purple ridges stretched away as far as the eye could see. Through them wound grey-green rivers, meandering slowly to some unseen destination. They had arrived at the summit. She had never really thought she would make it this far . . . but she had.

Then she gave a bitter little laugh. She had made a discovery. She knew now the game he had played.

'That was all a beastly act!' she said accusingly. 'You wouldn't have, would you? You just used it . . . to make me carry on . . .'

She stood helplessly in front of him, her pride in tatters. She could have accepted it, that he had only wanted her with a raw animal passion, that would have been understandable in the circumstances. But now she knew that even that had been counterfeit. He had not wanted her at all, and her own desires had all been for nothing. Thank God she had had the strength to resist them.

'You never intended making love to

me, back there, did you?' she insisted fiercely.

He looked down at her, a strange little smile tugging at the corners of his full lips. Then he shrugged.

'No Kate . . . you're right. But I had to think of something to get you moving. You're pretty tough. You don't scare that easy. But all the time you've been with me, you've been scared of what I might do. Well, I can tell you this. I don't force women. And I don't go in for casual relationships. You don't need to be afraid of me.'

She turned away from him before he could see the denial in her eyes. He still didn't understand. She hadn't been frightened of him. She was in love with him, but she was afraid of the hurt such love could bring.

'I hate you,' she gritted through clenched teeth.

5

That night they lit a fire. Kate ignored Matt as far as was humanly possible, but he took no notice and after a while it became ridiculous to keep it up, and so she helped him collect the twigs and small branches that were dry enough to burn. The matches still worked, and once the fire had taken hold he foraged further to bring back more fuel, until it was a real blaze.

'Serves two purposes,' he told her. 'Keeps us warm, and we'll need it. There's always the possibility that a plane might spot it.'

She acknowledged his remark with a brief smile, and spread the blankets out in front of the blaze. Matt disappeared, and came back carrying some long straight branches. He squatted by the flames and took out his knife.

Studying him surreptitiously Kate

thought how perfectly he fitted this environment. The indelible stamp of his origins was evident in his broad high cheekbones, and the black hair that tumbled over fiercely penetrating black eyes, as though tousled by the wind. But more than that, there was a stillness about him, a strength of purpose. As the firelight flickered, throwing patterns of light across his intent features, she wondered painfully which of the many beautiful and sophisticated women he knew would be waiting for him if he ever made it back. And what would such a woman think if she could see him now, unshaven and unkempt, fashioning a crude spear, sharpening its point in the hot ashes?

Kate watched his hands moving with strong, sure movements, and stirred uneasily, a flame of desire flickering as she remembered the feel of those hands not so long ago. The very memory made her tingle and burn, hating herself for the response he had made her feel, when all the time he had been tricking her, using his knowledge of her . . .

'You can't hunt in the dark,' she objected tartly. 'Part Indian you may be, but even you can't do that.'

'Not on my own,' he agreed. 'But with you to hold the torch, I can. Come on, leave the fire.'

She followed him reluctantly out of the circle of firelight into the darkness, carrying the torch.

'We'll have to go a little lower, back into the trees.'

'No . . . ' she pleaded, hating the thought of returning to the dank forest. 'Please Matt . . . I'm not hungry, really.'

He chuckled. 'Cat'll get your tongue, if you tell lies! We won't go far. Just a little way. We won't get lost.'

They were lucky. When she had nearly given up hope the arcing beam of her flashlight caught something moving at the base of a tree. Matt's arm shot up with the speed of lightning. There was a scuffling noise, and he leaped.

Kate flung herself forward too, falling over a threshing furry thing. In the dancing shaking circle of her light she saw the gleam of Matt's knife. He took the torch from her, and examined the catch. Kate turned away, sickened.

'We're lucky. It's a mountain wallaby, and it's unusual for it to be this high. It was looking for leaves and fruit.'

Kate didn't want to know. She didn't want to think about what it had been. Until now meat had been something that one bought in neat anonymous little parcels. But it was food. Food! That was all that was important. She knew it, and she knew that Matt was right; he recognized that to survive they had to kill. How little it took to return to the level of primitive man.

Going back to the fire was like going home. Kate huddled in her warm, freshly dried blanket while Matt skinned the wallaby and prepared the meal. By the time it was ready she was ravenous. No matter that the meat was half charred and half raw . . . no matter that it smelled like a burnt offering and tasted even worse . . . she devoured it hungrily, accepting avidly from Matt's fingers the morsels he hacked from the carcass. At last he called a halt. It hadn't been a very big animal, but there was a little left over for the next day . . . and they might not be as lucky again.

The fire burned, crackling and sending forth occasional showers of bright sparks. Kate licked her fingers regretfully, and yawned.

'You've got grease on your chin,' Matt murmured. He rubbed it off with his thumb, sliding it across her full lower lip in a movement so sensuous in its slow deliberate touch that Kate's insides churned. She would have been fooled into thinking it meant something, if he had not already made it so clear that he did not feel for her in that way. She drew back from him, sharply.

'Do you still hate me then?' he murmured.

112

She shook her head mutely, unable to trust her voice. How could she hate him? He had become a part of her. She could not imagine a time without him. But she would have to.

'So, we're friends?'

Friends! Was that what it was, when you were happy to be with someone . . . even here, even if this might be all you ever knew of them, all you ever could be to them? When you were ready to take any crumb of affection they might offer? 'Of course we're friends, Matt,' she muttered.

He touched her hand briefly. 'You'd better rest now,' he said softly. 'It's been a hard day. You've done fine.'

Only because of you! she thought sleepily. Almost before he had tucked her up, her head pillowed on a pile of moss, she drifted into sleep.

It didn't seem long before Kate woke again, shivering. Above her a million stars looked coldly down from a sky that covered the mountain like a giant bowl. The fire had burned low. She

113

edged over to it, and groped for some more sticks. Matt stirred. 'What are you doing?'

'I'm c . . . cold,' she stuttered.

'Here, let me.'

He flung more wood on the fire, and poked it back into a blaze. Then he spread his blanket over her. 'It'd be stupid to perish from cold, after all we've been through. You'll have to cuddle me tonight, Kate.'

She made no objection. Why should she? She was safe enough with him, he had made that abundantly clear . . . and besides which, she was too cold and too tired to care. She allowed him to pull her close, curling up behind her his knees tucked into hers, one arm around her waist. The fire had once more begun to send out warmth. It must be the fire that was causing a glow to spread through her.

When Kate woke again it was early morning. The blanket was wet with condensation, where it touched her face. Her head was pillowed on Matt's shoulder, and her hand ... Her eyes widened, and she cautiously experimented by flexing her fingers. Yes, she had not been mistaken — her free hand was tucked inside Matt's shirt. Had he put it there to warm, or had it crept in there of its own accord? She blushed at the thought, and tried to withdraw it without waking him. He stirred, and she paused, feeling the steady rise of the broad chest under her fingers, the abrasive roughness of hair beneath her palm. Carefully she pulled back her hand again, until it was free.

She raised herself up on one elbow. Although the air was still cold the day was bright. The short springy grass around them was soaked by a heavy dew, and so were their coverings. She looked down at Matt, and her mouth curved in a wistful smile. So tough, and yet so vulnerable. His beard was well under way now, black and wiry, and the droplets of dew caught in it sparkled in the morning sunlight. It made him seem more like a brigand than ever. Never could there be a man with more raw masculinity, but the lashes that hid those disturbingly direct eyes were as thick as a girl's, and his firm sensual lips curved sweetly.

Kate's eyes darkened, and her soft lips parted, as she fought down an urge to lower her head and cover his mouth with her own. She knew what would happen if she did. He would awake in a flash, and those strong arms would clasp her to him. Oh yes, he might not desire her, but he was man enough not to refuse what he would have every right to believe to be an invitation.

Matt stretched. Black eyes opened and stared penetratingly into hers. He made the transition from sleep to wakefulness quickly, like an animal, alert for any danger. 'Anything wrong?'

Kate gave a little laugh. What a question. He had turned her life topsyturvy. Her, Kate Summers, the girl who thought she had it all worked out — who had sworn never to put her heart at risk again, caught in the love-trap of a man who saw her only as an encumbrance. As if that was not enough, they had reached this ridge, but all around them lay a muted world of yellow-green and purple peaks that snatched at the wispy remnants of mist, and below them, she knew, lay the forests again.

'Oh no,' she said ironically. 'Everything's wonderful!'

'Good. Let's get going then.'

They packed with a speed that had now become habitual, and Kate followed him over the brow of the hill. It was not long before she was thinking back longingly to the camp they had just left. There had been something cosy and reassuring about it, almost domesticated. Trudging after Matt she reflected that in just such a way stone-age woman must have followed her man. How she had changed. She had become unsure of herself, more aware of herself in the one aspect most important to any real woman. She was in love with this strange man, and that had changed everything. How to cope with it was a different matter, because it was not going to get her anywhere. She knew. She had loved before . . .

The morning wore on, the landscape altering. The trees were tall again, but further apart. Fast, sparkling streams cascaded down the rock, impeding their progress, and they had to work their way along rocky ledges to avoid them. It was hard going, but Matt would not let her take it easy; he drove her relentlessly. She sighed and limped after him. Her feet were blistered and swollen, and her left leg was burning where it had been bitten by the leeches, but she was not going to tell Matt . . . she was enough of a burden to him, as it was.

He was a man, she decided wearily, who would shoulder everyone's burdens, if he knew they were there, but he was so strong himself that he didn't always allow for the weakness of others. All the same, a man you could depend on, as she had discovered. He would make a good father.

But that was none of her business, she told herself hastily. If all the reports were to be believed he had no intention of being tied down. And he didn't find her the least bit attractive. He had forced himself to pretend, just to keep her climbing. Poor him! she thought indignantly. She had never wanted to fall in love again — had had no intention of becoming involved — but all the same, it was galling to be found so wanting as a woman.

She struggled on, walking in his footsteps as he slashed a way through for her, so close behind him that she might have been tied to him by an invisible rope, her eyes glued to the muscled strength of his body. It was pathetic, she told herself sternly, to become so obsessed with a man as to let him turn one's whole world upside down. Where was her pride? Gone, she decided ruefully. Gone a long time ago.

They rested and fed when the sun was high in the sky. 'Do you *really* think we'll ever get out of this?' Kate asked listlessly. Her leg was throbbing, and she was tired, but above all she was weary of her own thoughts.

Matt gave her a long cool look, taking in her air of utter exhaustion, the weary set of her shoulders, her head with its magnificent mane of hair now matted and tangled, drooping forward. He squatted beside her on a rotting log. 'I've told you, we're heading in the right direction,' he said gently. 'Don't you believe me?'

She shrugged. 'I suppose so.'

He brushed the back of his hand against her cheek in a casual, affectionate gesture. 'What's the matter?'

Kate shook her head, staring doggedly at the leaf strewn ground. 'Nothing . . . I'm fine.'

He curled his fingers around her jaw, and turned her face to his. Kate swallowed convulsively. He was looking at her with such compassion in those deep, dark eyes, that she could not break away from his gaze. She was a mass of conflicting, whirling emotions, and she no longer had the strength to cope with them.

'What is it, Kate?' he insisted softly. 'What's wrong?'

Should she tell him the truth? What would he say if she blurted it out, like a love-sick schoolgirl? I'm in love with you and I can't handle it! Her lips quivered, and then she shook her head angrily.

'If you must know,' she snapped, 'my leg is hurting.'

'Why the devil didn't you say sooner?' he exploded.

His anger was the last straw. The tears that had been threatening for so long spilled over, and she cried like a child, openly and without reserve. He pulled her into his arms, stroking her hair, and she nestled against him, her arms twining around his neck.

'Kate . . . ssshh now. Hush, we'll be all right, I promise you. Trust me.'

She looked up at him, blue eyes swimming with tears, her lips trembling. 'I do trust you, Matt. Don't be angry.'

He recoiled as if she'd struck him. 'Angry!' he groaned. 'Oh God, Kate . . . '

He bent his head and kissed her. His lips took hers so gently that there was nothing to frighten or disturb, just a feeling of warmth and security. Under their soft pressure she drifted into a sea of delight, her feelings opening out like a flower opening to the sun. She was hardly aware that her hands were burying themselves in his thick hair, that her lips were parting under his. She just let herself float with the tide, trusting herself to him. And it was Matt who pulled away first, putting her gently from him.

'Let's look at your leg,' he said gruffly.

She sat bemused and speechless as he rolled up her trousers and examined her. She no longer felt the throbbing heat of infection. All she was conscious of was a sense of loss. He had comforted her as he would a child, she thought sadly. It had meant so little to him.

'It's no wonder your leg's burning,' he said. 'This wound's infected. I'll have to clean it out.' A quick glance at her face, and he thrust the brandy flask into her hands. 'Take a good swig, it's still half full.'

'I don't like it . . . ' she began.

'Do as you're told!' he ordered. The look he gave her, half-exasperated, half-amused, brooked no argument. 'Why do you have to fight me all the way, Kate?' he murmured as he bent to his task. 'You fight me, you fight yourself. But I'll win in the end, my girl. You'll see . . . now hold still.'

She quite believed him. He was determined to win through, to get her back to safety. Then he would be able to forget her, his responsibility ended. He would be able to turn with relief to more rewarding relationships. She tilted back her head and took a great swig from the flask. The alcohol burned her throat and made her cough, but it took her mind off the pain of his probing knife. She took another swig, and another . . .

When he'd finished he took the flask from her hands. 'I didn't mean you to finish the lot,' he said ruefully.

There were tears on Kate's cheeks, but a warm glow in her stomach. 'I didn't yell when you hurt.'

'No, you did not,' he agreed, pulling her to her feet. 'You're a good girl.'

She swayed against him, and smiled up into his eyes. 'Am I, Matt?' she whispered.

He shook his head in disbelief. 'You're sloshed,' he accused. 'That's what comes from drinking on an empty stomach.' He took her hand. 'Come on, Kate. Let's go.'

She was content to let him half-carry her. A warmth that was not entirely alcohol filled her body. She forgot the danger, the discomfort, even the fact that to him she was only an added responsibility like an injured bird, or . . . or a tree. She wondered what kind of tree she must be; nothing sturdy like a beech or an oak. Some kind of willow, perhaps. A weeping willow. She giggled at the thought.

'Kate, look!'

He stopped so suddenly, she cannoned into him. They had come to a ravine, where the water cut a sharp cleft through the rocks. It would have been impossible to cross, if it had not been for the narrow vine bridge.

'A bridge. A *bridge!*' she gasped. 'That means . . .'

'It means people, Kate. Come on.'

They almost ran to it, it was narrow and rickety, swinging dizzily across the chasm where they could see the water boiling below. 'You're not in a fit state,' Matt said bluntly. 'We'll wait until you've sobered up.'

'No, I'm all right. Please Matt,' she argued tearfully. 'Let's cross.'

In the end she got her own way, though Matt made her cross the bridge on her hands and knees, and she inched stubbornly along in front of him, careful not to look down, keeping her mind firmly on the thought that this bridge must surely lead to safety.

On the far side a narrow track led downwards to a cleft in the rocks, where water cascaded in a white curtain. Almost hidden behind the waterfall was a pool overhung by coloured flowering vines, beside an open space carpeted with grass.

'It's . . . oh, it's beautiful,' breathed Kate. Around them the trees lifted proud heads to a sky of cerulean blue, and clinging to the trees, amongst the vines and lianas, were masses of orchids, pure white, the cleanest, purest white she had ever seen. It made her realize just how disgustingly filthy she had become.

'I want a swim,' she called. 'Are you coming?'

Without a thought to modesty she scrambled out of her clothes. Matt started to strip too, but she couldn't

126

wait for him. He tried to stop her, but impulsively she knocked his hand away, and dived headlong into the water. The cold nearly took her breath away.

'Kate, you little fool!'

As she surfaced, gasping and shaking her head there was a splash beside her, and a hand grabbed her by the hair and yanked her back to the bank. Then Matt's arms were about her, lifting her up onto a grassy ledge, and he was lying beside her, leaning over her, his face taut with anxiety.

'You could have killed yourself!'

The water trickled down from his shoulders, catching in the dark expanse of his chest. Kate touched him tentatively. 'But I didn't,' she said softly, the alcohol still making her reckless. Her fingers crept up towards his shoulders, her eyes following with fascination the drops of water that slid over his warm brown skin.

He smoothed back her mane of hair, and his hand continued to glide softly down the curve of her back, sending a shiver of anticipation along her spine. 'No . . . ' he answered hoarsely, 'but you sure gave me a scare.'

It was true, she realized with surprise. His face still held a tortured look, and he was trembling. Instinctively she stretched out her arms and drew him to her. As their bodies touched the sudden flare of sensation made her gasp.

'Kate . . . you don't know what you're doing.' His voice was thick and uneven, his lips pressed against her throat. 'Oh God, I must . . . '

He kissed her neck, nuzzling, exploring her throat with his mouth and tongue as if he wanted to drink the very essence of her, and she was unable to protest, her limbs heavy with a longing that was building inside her. Languorously, she turned her head and buried her mouth in his hair, wet and dripping though it was. Then he raised his head and his eyes burned into hers for a second before he pulled her to him, his mouth taking hers fiercely as his hand cupped her breast.

She had no time to ask herself if she was being a fool; no chance to stifle her own response; sensation exploded hot and urgent inside her as she felt his skin wet and warm against hers. Kate opened her eyes for a second, and the forest spun, so she closed them, swept away by a force against which she was completely powerless, as his mouth claimed hers.

At last he relinquished her lips, and she gasped as he moved to trace a line of butterfly soft kisses down her throat and shoulders to her breasts, fastening his mouth on first one rosy tip and then the other, gently tugging them with his teeth, testing with a warm tongue until she cried out and squirmed with a pleasure that was almost a pain. Dimly she was aware of the roaring of the waterfall, the cool smell of the dark pool, the prickly softness of the grass on her naked back, but all these things receded and became nothing as she swirled into the vortex of yearning that made her cry out.

'Matt . . . oh Matt, please!'

Was she begging him to stop, or imploring him to feed the hunger that was so strong as to be a pain inside her? She hardly knew. And it didn't matter . . . because now he was drawing away from her, holding her by her arms, away from him.

'No . . . ' he gasped, and it came out like a groan. 'No, Kate.'

She stared at him, puzzled, staring up into the dark eyes that now held something like regret. That was it! It was her fault. She had been to blame. Yes, she had forced herself on a man who did not even want her. Hadn't he made that abundantly clear? 'You're quite safe with me,' he'd said. 'I don't go in for casual relationships.' What did he think of her now? She had flung herself at him, virtually seduced him. Another man would have taken her . . . but not Matt. He had his principles, he

130

would not take a woman he did not love.

A flood of scarlet spread up her neck and into her face as she remembered her own abandoned response, the delight she had taken in his lovemaking. Oh, how right she had been to be afraid of this man. How right to shrink away from what might be. Love could hurt. It was hurting now. Worse than it had with David . . . A sob broke from her lips.

'Kate . . . Kate, for God's sake what is it?' He was beside her, his arms reaching out, but she struck him away and scrambled to her feet, staring at him with eyes wild and desperate. 'Leave me alone,' she panted. 'Don't touch me!'

She turned and fled, not knowing where she was going, running like a hunted fawn, her naked unprotected body whipped by the branches as she plunged through the undergrowth, anywhere . . . anywhere to escape him.

He caught her before she had gone

too far, bringing her down with a rugby tackle that brought them both crashing to the ground, and then grabbing her, crushing her against his chest as he knelt beside her. She strained away, gasping and sobbing, but he would not let her go, and at last she subsided into quivering sighs, leaning against him.

'That's better,' he murmured, stroking her hair. He tried to look into her face, but she buried it in his shoulder, tasting her own tears salty against his skin, until he took hold of a handful of her hair and forced her head back and looked straight into her eyes.

His jaw was set, face dark and stern as he stared down at her. 'I'm not letting you get away with it this time, Kate,' he growled. 'We've got to have this thing out.'

'Please,' she begged faintly, wanting to close her eyes to block out his accusing gaze, but unable to look away. 'Matt . . . I'm sorry.'

His expression softened, amusement quirking his lips. 'Sorry? What should you be sorry about, except finishing off the brandy!'

She flushed. That was what he thought — that she had just been carried away, under the influence. Well, let him think that.

'I apologize for the way I behaved,' she said coldly. 'I . . . I'm not used to drink.'

He held her at arm's length, peering into her averted face. 'It's not just that though, is it sweetheart? You've been hurt. Badly hurt. Can't you tell me about it?'

Kate sat, silent. A brightly coloured bird flew out of the bushes, startling her. Matt steadied her, and she looked at him in surprise, as if she had forgotten where she was, and who she was with. Then she gave a long sigh, and sagged against him. 'There's not a lot to tell,' she told him. 'His name was David . . .'

6

Matt wrapped a blanket around her, and held her until she stopped shaking. 'Just you wait there, until I get a fire going.'

Once she was dressed and warmed, he took her hands in his. 'Come on now, Kate. Out with it.' He stroked her cheek with his finger, wiping away a tear that was trickling down. 'What did this David do, that it put you off men for life?'

She felt foolish: how did you tell anyone how it felt to find the man you loved had been using you; had never really wanted you; had thought of you as a means to an end? And all the worse since she had known him ever since childhood . . . or thought she had.

'We were to have been married,' she began haltingly. 'I had just turned eighteen at the time, and my parents were against it, even though they knew David well . . . ' Perhaps, she thought ruefully, they had known him better than she had, even then.

'Come on,' persisted Matt. 'What happened? Did he sweep you off your feet?'

Had he? She supposed he had. She had been a very young eighteen year old, more interested in art than in boys, but she had always had a crush on David. Ever since she could remember she had tagged on after him. He, of course, had not bothered with her, unless she could be of use to him. Even then . . .

'We knew each other since childhood,' she said carefully. 'Then I went to a boarding school that specialized in art, and David went abroad. His parents still lived near us, but we didn't know them very well at the time. David didn't write, of course. I . . . ' she coloured, this was sounding so silly. ' . . . I used to dream about the day he would come back.' And by the time he did, she had changed from a child, to a young woman. David had not been slow to notice.

Kate sighed, and leaned against Matt, looking up at the splashes of light that came through the foliage. 'It seemed as though all my prayers had been answered. I never asked where he had been, or what he had been doing. I was only too pleased that he had noticed me at last.'

'So the prodigal returned, and you fell into his arms?' Matt's voice held a hint of amusement. Kate flushed.

'You might say that,' she said stiffly. 'I was young, and he seemed very sophisticated to me. He began to date me. We talked a lot, and I was flattered that he took such an interest in me.' She turned her head away, gazing studiedly at the lake. 'I can see now that he was perhaps more interested in his prospects in my father's firm, than he was in me.'

'You mean, he saw his chances.'

She nodded. 'Oh yes. That was all it was. The wonderful job he was supposed to have had in Germany had disappeared . . . perhaps he had been thrown out, I never did learn the truth of it. On my suggestion father took him on. He did work hard, I'll give him that. But just being an employee was not enough for David. He had ambitions, and I was to play a prominent part in them. You see,' she said painfully, 'once I became eighteen I came into a large packet of shares in the family company, in my own right.'

Matt's eyebrows rose. 'Ah, I see it all now.'

Kate gave a short laugh. 'Yes . . . well, it's obvious isn't it. But it wasn't to me, not at the time. They tried to warn me, but I wouldn't listen. I couldn't believe them. I was so sure David loved me. Since they were so against it, we ran away to be married.'

'Hang on a minute,' said Matt.

'Surely that would have shot his chances in your father's firm?'

She shook her head. 'You don't know how clever he was. He had some money — goodness knows where it came from — and he'd been secretly buying up voting shares. Once we were married, he thought I would be under his thumb. He would get onto the Board. He figured Daddy wouldn't hurt me by throwing him out. He was a gambler, willing to take risks.'

She fell silent, remembering that day. A day she had tried so hard to forget. The way she had packed and slipped away, hardening her heart, rejoicing in the knowledge that she and David would soon be married. The journey to the register office. Standing there with David beside her, and then her parents bursting in . . .

'I was lucky,' she told Matt stiffly. 'They found us just in time. And they had someone else with them. David's wife.'

'His wife!' For once Matt was shaken

138

out of his customary calm. 'The little creep was married?'

'Oh yes. Very married. She had a child too.' Kate's voice was full of scorn, scorn for herself; for allowing herself to be used, for loving a man who had turned out to be so worthless. 'He had married her in Germany, under a false name, because she had insisted on it when she became pregnant. Then he ditched her. She was no use to him, you see. When he returned to England he thought she would never trace him.'

There was a long silence. Then, 'But that was a long time ago,' Matt said gently. 'You were barely more than a child.' He took hold of her by her shoulders and shook her, trying to force that blank, shocked look from her eyes. 'Don't you think it's time you stopped making a martyr of yourself over one stupid incident?'

Kate was catapulted into anger, cringing away from him. Her blue eyes darkened and flashed. 'How . . . how dare you!' she stammered.

139

'What would you know about it? I should have known better than to tell you *anything*.' A pain held her, worse than anything she'd known before. To dismiss the past so easily, to imply that it didn't matter! Only she could know how much it had mattered, how it had eaten into her whole life, spoiling every relationship she had ever made, like a worm eating into an apple.

'Well, damn it woman. Tell me why?' He was angry now too, shouting at her. 'You found out in time. All right, so your heart was broken. It happens all the time. What was so bad about it that it has to ruin your life?'

She drew back from him, her eyes blazing. 'It killed my father — that's what it did. The worry . . . the dash to the register office. He had a heart attack and died that very night. And my mother never forgave me. I don't blame her. She told me it was my fault. I had killed my father. She told me to get out of her sight. So I did. I left there and then. And I never saw her again.'

'Kate!' There was a note of desperation in his voice. She supposed he was wishing now that he had never got involved in all this. What man wants to find he has nearly bedded a neurotic woman with a guilt complex, knowing he is still responsible for her safety?

'I'm sorry,' she said jerkily, scrambling to her feet, 'for burdening you with all this. But you did ask . . .'

He stopped her with an almost imperceptible movement of his hand. 'Kate,' he murmured through lips strangely stiff. 'Your life story must wait; something has just bitten my leg.'

She didn't understand him at first, his words were so calm, so ordinary, but then the meaning sank through. 'Oh God! What d'you mean . . . where?' she gasped. She stared at the leafstrewn ground they were sitting on.

'It's gone,' he said, in almost a conversational tone. 'It was a snake.

141

Peachy-pink it was, with black bands.'

'Is that a dangerous one?'

He grimaced. 'I'd rather it hadn't taken a fancy to me.'

He took out his knife, and handed it to her, rolling over on to his face, burying his face on folded arms. 'Left leg, in the calf,' he told her. 'Slit the trouser, Kate. Hurry.'

Her own story was forgotten, irrelevant, devoid of meaning any more. Nothing mattered but the man lying in front of her. She sawed desperately at the trouser material, ripping it away from his leg, revealing his strong calf muscle where there was already a flushed area spreading from a double puncture mark.

'Now cut, Kate,' he ordered. 'Suck the wound, and then spit out. I'm sorry . . . ' he sounded almost amused. 'I'd do it myself, but I'm not a contortionist.'

Kate's fingers closed around the knife's handle. 'I . . . don't know if I can . . . ' she croaked.

'Do it!'

Kate took a deep breath, and pressed the tip of the knife against his calf where the snake had bitten. She placed her fingers over the blade, staring at it with painful intensity. Afraid that she would not be able to pierce the skin she jabbed hard, and felt Matt's body leap convulsively. She closed her eyes for a moment, and then opened them fearfully to see the blood welling up bright and thick.

'Strewth,' he groaned. 'You'll never make a surgeon!'

Ignoring the quip she bent her head. Three times she fastened her lips on the wound and sucked hard, until he stopped her. 'That should do. Cut off a creeper, Kate, and make a tourniquet . . . just above . . . about here.'

She obeyed as quickly as she could. He was sitting up now, but she didn't like the look of him. His breathing was fast, but he was calm, making her do everything he said methodically, without panic. 'Now, Kate. Lend me an arm, and we'll be on our way.' He hauled himself to his feet, but as he leaned on her he swayed and collapsed.

Kate looked at him anxiously. 'How are you feeling?'

His grin was devil-may-care, but she was quick to notice an over-brightness in his eyes, a flush coming up into his cheeks. The angry red part on his calf was getting bigger. 'Not very sexy at the moment, my love,' he joked. Then he closed his eyes.

He had called her his love. She noted that, even though she had no time to think about it at the moment. A wave of panic swept over Kate. Surely, surely nothing could happen to Matt. She pressed her face against his, and was alarmed at the heat she felt from his skin.

'What are we going to do?' she faltered.

He opened his eyes again. 'You, Kate. What *you* are going to do. You're going to keep on going down that path, as quick as you can. And you're going to find help.'

'Matt!' Her grip on him tightened. 'I won't leave you.' She felt tears trickling down her cheeks, almost as salty as his blood that she could still taste in her mouth.

He shook his dark head. 'You've got to press on alone. I'll be all right here, Kate. I promise.'

'No!' She pressed her lips against his thick hair, trying to keep the fear out of her voice. 'I'll stay with you until you feel better. It'll surely wear off soon . . .'

'Do you want to wait here for me to die?' he rasped.

She gasped. His eyes burned into hers. 'Go!' he shouted with what seemed to be the last of his strength. 'Get the hell out of here.' Then he fell back, unconscious.

Kate gathered him up against her, with a moan, rocking with his head against her chest. What was the use? Who was he fooling? He was sending her for help, knowing full well that by the time she found anyone it would be too late for him. There was only a slim chance that she would be saved, herself, but he had wanted her to take it, leaving him to die all alone . . .

She laid her cheek against his head, and wept. Matt had been right. She had wasted all those years, torturing herself over something that had happened in the past, afraid to live in the present. And now it was too late, and Matt would never know what he meant to her.

A twig cracked. Kate lifted her head, her eyes dull and red with weeping.

Feet . . . dusty feet all around her, and the shafts of long spears. With disbelief she looked higher. Eight men stood in a circle around her. One had a cloth tied around his middle, but the others were stark naked. They were silent, black eyes staring. Kate crouched there, not moving, staring wide-eyed back at them. Then one lifted his spear, and moved forward . . .

146

The morning river mists had long since cleared, and afternoon sunshine sparkled on the water as it frothed around the rocks near the river-bank and swirled into a safe pool where the village children played. Kate sighed with pleasure, and picked up her pencil and the last precious piece of sketching paper. It was wonderful to be able to relax, knowing that Matt was recovering fast. That terrible journey seemed years behind them: her initial fright; then her relief as the hunters had leaped into action. They had known what to do. One of them — the leader named Arutap — had chewed leaves, squirting a stream of juice into Matt's mouth. Primitive, but effective it seemed. Then they had carried him down the path to the river, and then by canoe to their village.

Arutap's wife Taku, and a toothless old crone, Supuk, had cared for him. Others had built them a crude hut a little way from the communal longhouse, and there Kate had stayed with him, nursing him night and day until he regained his strength . . . and all the time the village drums had been beating out the news of their whereabouts.

Matt was better now, no doubt about it. Only that morning she had attempted to bathe him, as she had done for the last few days, and he had grabbed her around the waist, laughing and holding her with surprising strength for a man who had been at death's door!

'Go back to sleep,' she had scolded. 'I want you fit by the time someone comes for us. It can't be long now. The drums have been sounding out for days.'

Then she had wandered to the river bank, where she had joined the women, washing her hair and her clothes, borrowing a red sarong-type garment from Taku, which she wrapped around herself, fastening it just above her breasts by tucking one end over another. Close by her Taku was bathing a wriggling brown baby, looking back over her shoulder at Kate with a shy giggle. Taku's eyes were shiny brown with clear whites, her cheeks plump, her full lips well defined with a sweet turn to them. Kate strove faithfully to record the flowing lines of her body, the play of light and shade on her naked shoulders, the twist of coloured cloth around her hips.

Supuk was there too, bossing all the other women, sitting bonily naked and as wrinkled as a prune, slapping her broad flat feet on the surface of the water, shouting gummy advice and admonitions to the playing infants in a cracked and strident voice. Seeing Kate she cackled, and called something.

'What did she say?'

Taku tittered. 'She say why you not with your man? You best medicine now.'

Yes, why wasn't she with him? Kate wondered. Why, when he had reached out for her, with the light of interest in his eyes, had she scolded him and run away? Did the past still have such a grip on her? She shook her head impatiently. It wasn't that, though Matt might be forgiven for imagining it was. She had thought a lot during her night watches. She had chased away the ghosts by bringing them out and examining them carefully, and he had been right. She had wasted the best part of her life agonizing over what was over and done with. She had resolved to put that part of her life behind her . . . so why run away?

Kate looked thoughtfully at her fingers trailing in the water. She was afraid. That was the truth of it, be honest now. She was afraid to admit that she loved Matt, because soon now he would be gone, and what had just been an episode to him would be the end of everything for her. So she was avoiding the issue, in the hope of not getting hurt. And in doing that, she told herself, I'm denying myself, and him too. Don't be such a damned fool!

With a decisive movement she rose to her feet, gathering up her dried clothes and her sketching materials, and tucking them under one arm. She waved a cheery goodbye to the village women, and walked back towards the little hut, her shoulders brown and bare under flowing hair that was now at least clean, even if still somewhat tangled. The sarong only reached to the top of her thighs, and she walked with graceful light steps. Her heart was lighter too, because she had just realized something she had been blind to before.

She had always imagined her chances with Matt Selby to be non-existent, but that had been because of her own mixed-up feelings. Now things were different. Now she could go to him and show him a new Kate Summers — the one, perhaps, that poor Evan had searched for so unsuccessfully. If she wanted Matt it was up to her to prove it to him. At the hut she halted for a moment. I want him, she said to herself. It must be all right this time. Bending down she picked one of the white orchids that grew in prolific beauty at her feet.

Matt was fast asleep. Kate paused, unsure of herself. Trust Matt to be asleep, when she had screwed up her courage to come to him, her heart in her hands! He was lying on his back, one knee drawn slightly up, his hands behind his head, the sun filtering through the bamboo slats of the hut making criss-cross patterns on his bare skin.

She laid down her burdens quietly, and knelt beside him. The journey through the jungle, the lack of food, and his illness had made its mark on him, as it had on her. There were purple bruises where the leeches had fastened, and lacerations from the thorns. But even so, his body was beautiful. So strong and clean-limbed. She touched his chest, the curly dark hair abrasive against her hand. She ran her fingers down his ribs, now showing rather too well, to the flatness of his stomach. Her lips curved in a smile. Men were strange things, come to think of it, so strong when aroused, so defenceless when relaxed!

Reaching out she picked up the orchid she had abandoned, and placed it strategically. Then, sitting back on her heels she considered the effect, and chuckled.

Matt opened his eyes, waking without moving a muscle, as he always did. His eyes were glittering pools of darkness, his face expressionless, as if he were holding himself in check. Kate bent forward to taste the warmth of his lips. The feel of them sent a shiver of anticipation through her, but as soon as she felt them open and respond, she drew away. Matt lay silent, his eyes fixed on her face, and she gave him a slight reassuring smile before she stooped again, and fixed her lips against the skin of his shoulder.

'Oh God, Kate,' he groaned. 'D'you

know what you're doing? Are you going to run off screaming again?'

Kate straightened up, and smiled into his eyes. 'Not this time,' she whispered. Curling her fingers around his she lifted his hand and laid it on her breast.

'Kate . . . ?' There was a question in his voice, as he reached out to cup both her breasts in his hands, as if savouring the feel of their weight on his palms. She closed her eyes as his thumbs began a rhythmic stroking, letting her head fall back with an abandoned gesture.

'Your body is so beautiful.' The words were almost a whisper, but she heard them.

'Scratched, and battered, and scarred and . . . '

'That doesn't matter; that's surface only. You're beautiful. Beautiful all through.'

'I'm glad,' she said huskily. 'Kiss me, Matt.'

'Kate . . . ' The cry seemed forced

out of him, and he gripped her tightly, raining kisses on her, touching her, tasting her, as if he could not get enough. Then suddenly he drew away.

'What's the matter, Matt? Wasn't I . . . I mean, wasn't it . . . ' she broke off, suddenly appalled. Perhaps she had been wrong. He didn't really want her. She flushed, feeling a wave of red sweep up her neck and into her face.

Kate turned her face away sharply, her hair swinging. 'I'm sorry!' She gave a brittle laugh. 'I always seem to jump to the wrong conclusions, don't I? It's just . . . '

'Oh, Kate!' He put one hand under her chin, forcing her to look at him. 'Don't be a silly goose. It's simply . . . I was wondering . . . why? To rid yourself of the past? To prove something to yourself? Am I a dose of medicine, unpleasant but necessary to get rid of the symptoms?'

So that was it! Kate laughed aloud with relief. How could he think it . . . how could he even imagine such a thing? Wasn't it patently obvious to him that she was in love with him, crazily, ridiculously, and completely in love? Well, never mind, however he got such a silly idea into his head, it was something she could put right quite easily. She put out a hand, and touched his face tenderly.

'Some medicine,' she murmured. 'Believe me, if all medicine was like that, I could become an addict! But listen to me, Matt Selby . . . I want to tell you . . .'

But what she had to tell him was never uttered, because she was interrupted by such a commotion outside the hut that Matt hushed her, sitting bolt upright, tense, listening to the babble of voices. Then the hunter Arutap stuck his face through the hut opening.

'Come. You come quick. Men come.' He disappeared.

'That is it!' Matt sprang to his feet, and pulled Kate up with him. He was laughing, excited. 'This is it, Kate. They've come for us. We're being rescued.'

'Oh Matt, are you sure?'

They hung together, hugging and laughing. Then he began pulling on his trousers. By the time they broke out into the brightness of the sunlight, the whole village was gathered by the riverside, and as they ran to join them the ranks of dark bodies parted to give way to two white men who walked towards them. The first one held out his hand. 'Harold Mitchell. I say, we just couldn't believe it when the news arrived. We'd given you all up. How many of you survived?'

'Just the two of us. God . . . are we pleased to see you!'

7

Everyone was talking at once. Harold Mitchell was asking Matt details of the whereabouts of the plane to relay to the proper authorities.

'Does it feel strange,' asked the other, grey-haired man, 'to be rescued, I mean? I suppose you'd begun to wonder if you'd ever see civilization again.'

'Not once we reached the village,' said Kate. 'I knew then that we were safe. Just a matter of time.' She stopped speaking, and just stood there, watching Matt. All around them the villagers were crowding, eager not to miss anything. She caught Taku's eye.

'You goin' now?' asked the girl.

'Well, yes, I suppose so, Taku.' Kate turned to Harold Mitchell. 'Are you taking us now? How did you travel?'

He smiled. 'So many questions. Yes, I reckon we'll start back straight away. We'll go by boat for part of the journey, and then by helicopter. There's a clearing in the forest down river, and the 'copter's waiting there.'

'And where are you taking us?' To her own surprise Kate found that she didn't really care. All she wanted was to find a few minutes to talk to Matt. For so many days now there had been just the two of them, forced into an intimacy that had blossomed — for her part at least — into love. And now there were so many people around that Matt could not even spare her a glance. All the same, she was pleased when she learned they would be going to Wiatapi.

'It's the nearest place with proper facilities,' the man explained. 'There'll be a doctor there to check you over.'

'Oh, no need for that,' said Kate vaguely. 'There's nothing wrong with us.' Nothing wrong with me, she thought, but a horrible feeling of uncertainty. Oh, she was pleased to be rescued. Of course she was. It was just, why did they have to turn up at that particular moment? Couldn't they have come just a little later, a day, or even a few hours? Then she might have known exactly what she did mean to Matt. As it was, she felt free of the past and yet adrift on a new sea of emotions that were equally disturbing. Still, there would be time, she supposed, once they reached Wiatapi. Time to spend sorting themselves out, finding out just what place they had in each other's lives.

'Will you get your things together?' asked Harold Mitchell. Kate looked at Matt who grinned back at her, and for one moment his glance held all their shared memories.

'We . . . er . . . didn't bring much luggage.'

'I have my sketches,' explained Kate, with a smile.

'And two blankets,' added Matt. 'I suppose strictly speaking they belong to the airline, but I don't suppose they'll miss them if I leave them with Supuk and Arutap.'

There were goodbyes to be said, and the whole village followed them down to the sturdy river-boat with its outboard motor. Kate looked back at the little hut, standing on its own away from the long-house. She felt as if she were leaving a very important part of herself there. Then they cast off from the bank.

'Katee fella, you come back by 'm by,' shouted Taku before a bend in the river hid them from sight.

Would she ever see them again? It was doubtful. Kate reproached herself for not feeling more grateful for their rescue. It was what they had hoped for, dreamed about, every moment since the plane crash, wasn't it? At least Matt looked pleased enough for the two of them, she reflected uneasily. His thoughts must already be winging ahead to happy reunions, he was so busy chatting to Harold Mitchell that he had hardly spared her more than a glance and a squeeze of her shoulder as he pushed past her to sit in the bow of the boat.

The journey was uneventful. Kate sat near the stern of the boat next to the man called Peter. He was talkative. Too talkative. Kate found it hard to answer questions.

'I'm sorry,' she apologized awkwardly. 'I know I'm not being very forthcoming, but it's just . . . '

'I understand,' he assured her, but she doubted if he did. 'Mind you,' he added. 'You'll have quite a reception waiting for you at Wiatapi.'

Kate didn't understand. 'Airport officials?'

He laughed. 'You don't realize, do you? The world's press, my dear. You are celebrities now.'

'Did you hear that Matt?' she called over the noise of the outboard motor. 'We're famous.'

'So long as I can have a hot bath, and a long cold drink, I couldn't care less.' He flashed Kate a grin. 'And you might be able to find a comb at Wiatapi, though quite what you'll do with that mop of yours, I don't know.'

She laughed, but it rang false. She was becoming acutely conscious of her appearance, of her shaggy and matted hair, of her scratches and bruises, and the state of her clothes, soon to be exposed to the curiosity of the public. Matt looked romantically dishevelled, but she only looked a mess.

She felt even more nervous when they reached the landing point, and boarded the helicopter, but after a few seconds she found it fascinating to look down on the dark green canopy of the forest and wonder just where it was that she and Matt had fought their way through thorns; had been pestered by flies, devoured by leeches. Where was the waterfall? From the air it all appeared the same.

When the lodge at Wiatapi came into view it looked like a doll's-house, set in an oasis of gardens that held the jungle at arm's length. From it paths meandered off in all directions; a little way to the north there was the glint of a lake. The lodge itself was long and low, with an ornately thatched roof that soared upwards, curved peaks at either end. As the helicopter dropped lower Kate could see that the walls of the house were of wood, carved and patterned, and the front jutted out beneath the overhanging thatch.

It was from this veranda that the people came pouring, spilling out in a dark stream across the neatly cut lawns, like so many ants.

'They've been waiting for us,' said Harold Mitchell. 'All the cameras at the ready. You'll be on T.V. tonight.'

They dropped lower still, and almost at the last minute, the crowds drew back to allow them to land. Kate could distinguish faces now, but it was too overwhelming for her to pick out any one person. In any case, there would be nobody there she knew. She resented being pinned down like a specimen, to be goggled over in the next morning's papers.

With a slight bump the helicopter settled. 'Out you get,' said Peter. 'Keep your head down, mind the blades.'

Matt jumped down ahead of her, and handed her down, tucking his hand under her elbow, urging her forward. Immediately they were surrounded by a battery of reporters.

'Miss Summers, how does it feel to be rescued?'

'It feels good,' stammered Kate.

'Can you tell us what happened?'

'How long were you at the village?'

'What happened to the other passengers?'

Matt continued to propel her towards the house. 'Let us through,' he shouted. 'We'll make a statement later.'

'Miss Summers, how did you feel when you crashed?'

'Oh . . . terrified, I guess.'

'Would you say that Mr. Selby saved your life?'

Kate glanced sideways at Matt. He

seemed to be coping better than she was. 'Well . . . yes. Yes, of course, I could never have got through without him.'

'Could you tell us . . . ?'

'How did you feel . . . ?'

Then she heard a different voice, one she knew well. 'Kate! Kate, thank God you're alive!'

She stood on tiptoe, to see over the milling heads. Evan? Yes, she hadn't been mistaken. There was Evan, his face wreathed in smiles, and he was struggling to reach her.

'Will you let me through please,' he was shouting. 'Excuse me. I must get through. Damn it all . . . let me through. That's my fiancée you're pestering!'

A way miraculously cleared, and more cameras clicked and flashed as she found herself separated from Matt.

'Kate, sweetheart. My God, what's been happening to you?'

She hugged him back, pleased to see him and touched by his obvious concern, but embarrassed by his greeting. But she shouldn't feel like that. He had only said it in order to reach her. It was natural. After all, they had known one another a long time, and of course he had been worried. All the same, she strained to see Matt.

Then to her dismay she saw him being swept away from her, surrounded by a group of journalists. For a moment he looked back over his shoulder, eyes dark and blazing, before stalking off towards the house.

'Matt!' she shouted. 'Wait a minute.'

She began to struggle through the crowd, using her elbows where necessary. 'I'm sorry, Evan — I must speak to Matt.'

She had to see him. Had to explain. Had to wipe away the dark expression of accusation that had been written so clearly on his features.

'Matt . . . please wait.'

But before she could reach him he was swallowed up into the house. Evan was by her side. 'Don't worry. You can see him later. Plenty of time. Come along, let's get you inside.'

Evan extricated her from the persistence of the journalists, spoke a word or two of thanks to Harold Mitchell and Peter, and urged her into the lodge. Kate was too exhausted to do anything except go along meekly. A man — she imagined it must be the manager — murmured words of congratulations and suggested she might like to retire to her room.

'Yes, come along,' said Evan. 'The best thing for you, a bit of peace. You look as if you need a rest and a good square meal. And anyway, there's somebody there waiting.'

'Oh Evan, no!' wailed Kate. 'Not somebody else.'

But he ignored her objections, and hurried her along. 'Here we are. This is your room. In you go, Kate. I'm going to leave you now for a little while. I'll see you later.'

Kate was puzzled. He had been so thrilled to see her, and yet now he was going to vanish, leaving her to the mercies of yet another well-wisher? She shrugged wearily. What did it matter? She would get rid of whoever it was quickly, and then all she wanted was a quick bath before she went to find Matt. She had to find him. She couldn't leave it like this, with him imagining goodness knows what.

Evan opened the door and pushed her into her room. 'Here she is, Veronica,' he said, and then withdrew.

A woman was standing beside her bed, one hand nervously plucking at a locket that hung around her neck. 'Kate . . . ' she whispered. 'Thank God.'

'Mother!'

This last shock simply broke Kate down. With a sob she collapsed into her mother's arms.

'Hush, don't cry, It's all right. You're safe now. Don't cry, Kate. Hush, hush my dear. It's all right.'

It was some time before Kate recovered enough to dry her eyes. 'I still can't believe it,' she sniffed, wiping her eyes on the back of her hand. Her mother laughed, and handed her the handkerchief with which she had been mopping her own.

'Let me look at you.'

They both sat on the edge of the single bed. 'You've grown up,' said Veronica, a catch in her voice.

Kate laughed tremulously. 'I'm twenty-six, Mother.'

Her mother's eyes filled with tears again. 'All those years wasted. Why did you leave, without a word?'

Nervously Kate traced the pattern on the bedspread with a shaking finger. Blue and green it was, to match the long pleated curtains. 'I couldn't face you any more. Knowing how you felt. I knew how angry you were with me . . . '

'With *you!* Oh, Kate . . . '

'And then,' Kate continued with an effort. 'You said . . . you said it was my fault that father died. And you were right. It *was* my fault . . . '

'I know what I said. Don't you

think I've cursed myself ever since. But people say things, Kate, when they are angry and hurt. Things they don't mean.'

Kate tore her eyes away from the intricate pattern, and looked her mother square in the face. It was true. There were no signs of anger or bitterness in those eyes, still brilliantly blue. If it was strange for her mother to discover a grown-up daughter, it was equally strange for her to find a mother who had become . . . well, more motherly.

'You've changed too,' she ventured.

Veronica laughed. 'I'm older too, you know. You needn't remind me.'

'No . . . ' said Kate slowly. 'You're just as lovely, but in a different way. More relaxed, more . . . '

'Happy? Yes, well, that's George's doing. I'm married again, Kate, to the dearest man in the world. Not that he'd replace your father. But, a dear man all the same. As soon as George heard about you, he insisted we fly out. We've rented a house in Sydney. Then

I flew on here to wait.'

Kate closed her eyes. 'Oh, there's so much to take in, my head's in a whirl.'

Her mother's smile faded as she took in the shadows under Kate's eyes, the torn clothing, and obvious signs of fatigue. 'I shouldn't have sprung it on you like this. You need to rest. Shall I order you a meal, or . . .'

'First,' said Kate, 'I want a bath.'

★ ★ ★

After the bath, her mother tucked her into bed, and there she was visited by the doctor who gave her a thorough examination, and pronounced her pretty fit, considering. 'All the same, young lady,' he said, packing away his stethoscope, 'I prescribe a long rest. Take it easy for a while. Your nervous system has taken quite a battering, these last few days, to say nothing of the physical strain.'

'Don't worry, doctor,' said her

mother. 'She's coming back to Sydney with me, to recuperate.'

It was the first Kate had heard of it. 'But mother . . .'

'Good,' said the doctor. 'I'll give you some ointment for those sores. You can collect it from the reception desk. Goodbye, Miss Summers. You're a very lucky young woman.'

He had no sooner left than Evan arrived, with a tray. Dear Evan. 'Are you both trying to fatten me up?' she asked in horror. 'I can't eat all this.'

'It's only a normal meal,' objected Evan. 'Really Kate . . .'

'It looks vast to me,' Kate muttered. She wouldn't harrow them by revealing what she had been eating lately. Not yet. To please them she made an effort, but she kept yawning. 'I'm sorry,' she said, blinking at them owlishly. 'I can't seem to keep my eyes open.'

'It's not surprising,' said her mother. She removed the tray, and settled Kate back into the bed, pulling the covers up. 'Go to sleep now.'

'But I must see Matt,' murmured Kate, in a comfortable haze. 'There's something I have to explain . . .'

'He'll be there in the morning,' said Evan. 'In any case, he'll be pretty busy just now. There's so much the authorities want to know. He's dealing with all that. Go to sleep now, there's a good girl.'

They left her, and Kate was aware of her mother's gentle touch on her hair, before the light went out, and the door closed. The bed was so comfortable. So much had happened. It was hard to think about it all: her mother; Evan; and Matt. In the morning she would see Matt. She would explain that Evan was only a dear friend. He would understand. In the morning she would put things right . . .

★ ★ ★

In fact, it was nearly lunchtime before she woke, and even then it was a struggle to open her eyes. She wondered

174

whether there had been something to sedate her in the milky drink last night, or perhaps it was just the pleasure of sleeping in a comfortable bed once more, secure and safe.

She found clothes laid out for her, her own clothes — she supposed Evan must have organized that, persuading the landlord of her flat to let him in to collect her things. Or perhaps it was her mother's doing.

As she washed and dressed she pondered on this new development. It was wonderful to have a mother again, and to find that the past was forgiven. Not forgotten . . . no, it could never be that. One could not recapture those years. They were both quite different people. It would take time.

And then, there was this business of going to Sydney. Her mother meant well, thought Kate, but it just wasn't on to take over her life like that. She didn't want to leave Wiatapi just yet. There was the job she had come here to do, and there was Matt . . .

The thought of him brought a flush to her cheeks, a quickening of her pulse. Was it barely a day since she had virtually seduced him in that little palm-covered hut? Already it seemed a little unreal, and she didn't want that. She wanted him there, with her, looking at her with those penetrating eyes filled with love . . . not with scorn, as he had looked at her yesterday. Did he think she had been lying to him? It must have seemed odd. She had told him that nobody cared about her, and yet the moment they returned there was a man waiting to claim her as his fiancée!

She looked at herself critically in the dressing table mirror. Matt would hardly recognize her today in this crisp white blouse and deep blue skirt. She turned sideways. The waistband was a little loose, she had certainly lost weight, but perhaps that wasn't a bad thing. It suited her to be a little thinner, accentuated those already high cheekbones, fined down her features.

Her mother had spent ages combing through her hair last night, that was probably why she had become so tired, but it had been worth it. Freshly washed, it stood out from her head in a pale cloud of crinkly waves. It was nice to feel something like attractive again, it gave her more confidence for when she had to confront Matt.

A tap at the door, and her mother entered. 'Ah, so you're up.' She nodded, smiling. 'You do look more human today. Feel like a spot of lunch in the dining-room?'

'Well, yes of course. But first, mother, I do want to see Matt. You don't understand . . .'

'But of course I do.' Her mother's eyes twinkled. 'I must say you picked the most attractive man to crash with. I wouldn't have minded being marooned with him at your age.'

She flushed. 'He saved my life.'

'Yes,' said Veronica gently. 'And I'm very grateful to him, as I'm sure you are. I expect he will be in the dining-room. If not, you can ask at the reception desk.'

But he was not in the dining-room. When she asked she was told that he had not yet put in an appearance, so, expecting that he would arrive at any moment, she joined her mother and Evan. The dining-room was large and airy, and their table was set in a window alcove, looking out onto the grass where the helicopter had landed the previous day. The journalists seemed to have disappeared, whether this meant that the story was no longer news, or whether the management had locked them out, she neither knew nor cared.

'Thank you for fetching my clothes, Evan.'

He went pink. 'Your mother helped there.'

Kate laughed. 'I thought she must have. Otherwise, there is no knowing what I would be wearing.'

'You look very pretty, anyway,' said Veronica. 'Doesn't she, Evan?'

'Stunning.'

Kate looked at him warily. His tone had been ardent. When he had left her in Sydney he had been adopting a 'take-it-or-leave-it' attitude, but the drama of her disappearance and then the rescue must have awakened all his former feelings.

While they ordered their meal and awaited its arrival Kate kept looking at the entrance to the dining-room. People were taking their places at the tables, but there was no sign of Matt. What was taking him so long? Wasn't he the slightest bit interested in how she was?

The food arrived. Kate had ordered steak, with a crispy side-salad. She ate slowly and with enjoyment, but with her mind elsewhere.

'What's that noise?' asked Veronica. There was a loud buzzing sound coming from outside. 'It's another helicopter,' said Evan.

From over the trees it came, a white one with lettering on the side. It hovered over them before coming in to land. This is what it must have been like yesterday, thought Kate, waiting for us to come in. People were crossing the room to peer out of the windows at it.

'W.C.C. World Conservation Congress,' said Evan, reading the logo on the side of the machine. 'I suppose it's come for Matt Selby. Pretty important he is, I guess.'

'Yes, I believe so,' Kate responded automatically. A woman was climbing out of the helicopter, a very beautiful woman, Kate could see that much, even at a distance. She was tall and slender, dressed in a sparkling white jump-suit, jet-black hair coiled around her head. Kate pushed back her chair. 'Excuse me,' she muttered, and fled the room.

The penny had suddenly dropped. The helicopter had come for Matt, and that meant he must be leaving. At any minute . . . leaving . . . and he had not tried to contact her, had not spared her a word. Well, it wasn't good enough. He *couldn't* just vanish out of her life without a word. Kate burst out of the lodge, and ran the length of the verandah. Yes, there he was, and he had suitcases with him.

'Matt!' she shouted. 'Matt, wait . . .'

He turned as she reached him, but there was no smile. His face was hard, impersonal. 'Yes, Miss Summers?' Polite enquiry. Otherwise, nothing.

Her eyes searched his face, aware of the woman in white who was advancing towards them. 'You were going to leave? Without saying goodbye?'

He looked down his nose at her, his lip curling. 'I thought you would naturally be otherwise engaged. After all, it isn't every day a girl is restored to the arms of a lover who had thought her dead.'

'But Matt . . .' The woman had nearly reached them, 'I wanted to explain,' hissed Kate furiously.

'No need,' he sneered. 'I'm not doubting you had problems, Kate.

I hope your fiancé appreciates the 'therapy' I gave.'

'Don't be stupid. I . . . '

'Matt . . . you devil!' She was there, the vision in white, an olive face and curving red lips, flinging her arms around Matt, her eyes full of obvious adoration. And there Matt was, hugging her back with just as obvious enthusiasm.

Kate stood rooted to the spot, until the ecstatic meeting was over, and the woman turned to her with a smile. 'You must be Kate Summers. I'm so glad Matt was there to bring you safely back.'

Kate could feel the colour draining from her face. 'Thank you,' she said through lips that were stiff. 'Matt, I just wanted to thank you, for everything.'

Was it her imagination, or was there a flicker of some emotion in his hard black eyes? He gave a slight bow. 'It was *my* pleasure.' The emphasis was insulting. 'I would have done the same for anyone!'

She stood there frozen while they walked away from her, Matt's arm around the woman's waist. Kate knew now where she had seen her before, in the background of many of those newspaper photographs. And then the helicopter took off, and she watched it rise and swing sideways over the trees, towards the coast. She watched it, until it completely disappeared from view.

'Did you manage to speak to him?' asked Veronica, when Kate rejoined them at the table.

'Yes,' said Kate, picking numbly at her meal. 'I said all there was to say.'

Later, she agreed to travel back to Sydney with her mother. For a while at least, to recuperate, and to allow them to get to know each other a little better. Eventually she would return here, she had to in order to finish the task she had set herself . . . but not yet. She needed time to sort herself out. She felt completely hollow. How could it end like this? How could Matt walk out of her life, as if nothing had ever happened?

Well, she thought dully, that question was easily answered. She saw that she had jumped to a lot of unwarranted assumptions. I don't go in for casual relationships. She had taken that to mean that he was not involved with anyone, but he had not actually said so. What he must have meant was that back home he had someone who was really important to him. And the woman in white *was* important. It had been plain on his face for anyone to see.

Her face began to burn. He had just been kind to her, stopping her from making a complete fool of herself . . . and now he was convinced she had just been using him!

'Come along,' said Veronica. 'Let's get packed up. The sooner we get to Sydney the better. You're still looking very peaky, you know. And George will be waiting.'

At least, thought Kate, I've found my mother. Hopefully everything would be all right between them from now on. 'Yes, mother,' she said gaily, striving with desperation to look as happy as she felt she ought to. 'Let's go home.'

8

Kate leaned forward and dabbed a brushful of burnt ochre at a painting of Taku on which she had been working for some days. She frowned, and swivelling around in her seat picked up a mirror and looked at her work as it was reflected in the glass. She often used that trick, to distance her from the easel, giving her a better idea of how it would look if she was standing further away.

In fact, it wasn't bad at all. It had something, something special, something that had been lacking in her earlier work. Taku's face laughed back at her, brown skin gleaming with a healthy sheen, the bright primary colours of her sarong standing out against the background greenery. Yes . . . it was good. Kate knew it, and *still* she wasn't satisfied. Holding the brush between her teeth she picked up a paint smeared cloth, and dabbed with irritation at the picture. Then she loaded the brush with paint again, and leaned forward once more.

'Damn!' With a flurry of temper she flung the brush across the room, where it skidded across the polished cork tiles. With a sigh she wiped her fingers and then rose from her painter's chair. Enough of that, she thought guiltily. Her mother and new stepfather had been more than kind. It was hardly fair to mess the place up in a fit of pique. And why was she feeling this way? Because she could not get a man out of her mind. A man with a hard-boned face and black hair that fell all ways. A man who could be aggravatingly tough, and yet disconcertingly gentle . . . and who was not in the least interested in her.

Angry with herself, she retrieved the brush, and cleaned up the few specks of yellow that stained the polished floor. Then she set about cleaning her brushes and putting them in place, ready for the next work session. She might as well give up for now, it was obvious that she wasn't going to achieve anything while she was in such a jangled state.

It was a pleasant room they had given her. Originally intended as a games room, it had a high, raftered ceiling and big picture-windows looking onto a pergola-covered patio. It was light and spacious, and held only her easel and stool, some shelves for paints and other materials, and a comfortable, squashy sofa where she could rest when she simply wanted to sit and think . . . she'd been doing far too much of that lately. It was time she stopped.

When they'd left Wiatapi she had thought she could return to a normal life, but it had not been that easy. The press, having been rebuffed at the Lodge, tracked her down on her arrival at the rented house near Sydney, and would have invaded the privacy of Veronica and George's home, if George had not sent them packing with a flea in their ear, and a formal complaint to the newspaper concerned. Eventually they were left in peace. Even so, there had been official enquiries to satisfy, and even some pathetic letters from relatives of those who had not survived the crash. Those she had answered personally, and she hoped that she had brought some comfort to the writers, but it had not been easy.

At last the interest had died down. Kate found that she was more tired than she had realized. Apart from nightmares about the plane, she had other dreams — dreams she did not want to admit to herself, but which left her crying into her pillow in the morning. And it just had to stop! She had made a fool of herself over a man. So what? She seemed to be making a habit of it, but at least Matt had made her face up to the deep seated guilt-complex that had bedevilled her for so long. Where she had gone wrong was to imagine that it had meant anything to him. She had to accept that. She would never see him again.

At least, this was a lovely place to recuperate. Like most of the houses here, it was single-storied, on a large plot of land. It was not far from the beach, and the vegetation was lush and green, proof of constant watering. From the shady patio wafted in the scent of flowering shrubs and eucalyptus trees.

Kate placed her brushes upright in the bright-blue mug her mother had provided, and wandered aimlessly to the window, wiping her fingers on her smock. Outside, the sprinklers were whirling plumes of water droplets onto the buffalo grass lawn. Nearer, the rafters of the flower-laden pergola cast deep shadows on the bricks of the patio. She could just catch a glimpse of Veronica's grey hair against the reclining sun-lounger. A hand stretched out and lifted a glass from a table. Her mother was taking a rest.

A tap at the door and George's face peered hesitantly around the door. 'Am

I interrupting anything vital?'

'No, you're not,' Kate sighed. 'I'd just given up for the day. I can't seem to get anything right.'

'What you need is a nice long cold drink. Will you join us on the patio?'

'I'd love to.'

George ventured further into the room, and stood looking at Taku's portrait, head on one side. 'Looks good to me, not that I'm any judge.'

Kate thoroughly approved of her mother's choice of a man. He was just what Veronica needed, solid, reliable, kind — but not dull. You could even say he was good-looking in a bluff, sunburned way. In fact, she realized with surprise, he was very much what her own father would have become, had he lived. Perhaps that had something to do with her mother's choice.

She shrugged. 'I can't seem to settle to anything. I don't know what's wrong with me. Usually, once I start working, I can lose myself completely.'

He placed a heavy hand on her

shoulder. 'Don't you think you're being a little hard on yourself? In the jungle you were simply trying to survive. Now you are safe, and reaction has set in. Ordinary life seems a little unreal, doesn't it?' He removed his hand and moved to the window. 'I know, because that's how I felt after the war. I was a prisoner-of-war for a time. I remember thinking, when I came home . . . I shall wake up in a minute.'

'Yes,' admitted Kate slowly. 'That's just how I do feel.'

'And another thing,' said George. He cleared his throat. 'Er . . . I just want to say how grateful I am that you agreed to come here. It has meant so much to your mother. I know perhaps she fusses over you a bit too much, and after managing your own life for so long, perhaps you long to be up and doing things again . . . but it has been so good for her. It has allowed her to get rid of her sense of guilt about all that business long ago.'

'*Her* sense of guilt?' Kate was

startled. She had become used to bearing the burden of what she imagined to be her own guilt, all these years. The idea of her mother feeling that way came as a shock.

'Of course, guilt,' said George gruffly. 'What d'you expect? In her eyes it was all her fault. You running off like that . . . she felt she should never have said what she did.'

George wheeled around, and beamed at her, glad to have that over with. 'Enough of that, eh? How about that drink? Go and join your mother, and I'll bring it out.'

On the patio Veronica greeted her with touching eagerness, pushing her sunglasses up onto her forehead. 'Oh, *there* you are. I was hoping you'd come out, but I didn't dare interrupt the genius at work.'

'Some genius!' sighed Kate, flopping into a sun-lounger. 'Nothing's going right.' She closed her eyes, and murmured appreciatively as the sun began to soak in. 'Mmmm. It's lovely out here. How wise you are, mother, just to relax and enjoy life.'

'But that doesn't suit you, does it?' Kate opened her eyes, to see her mother looking at her shrewdly. 'Now, you don't fool me, Kate. I'm too old a bird not to know when a girl's unhappy. Is it that nice man? He *is* sweet, but not quite right for you, I think . . . '

Kate looked bewildered. In no way was Matt sweet.

'Mother, who . . . ?'

'Evan. Who else would I be talking about? Is that why you are like a cat on hot bricks?'

Kate was glad to be able to laugh and answer quite honestly. 'No — nothing like that. Evan and I are old friends. That's all. Evan is very conventional. A woman who gets herself marooned in a rain forest is not really an ideal wife for him.'

'Hmmm.' Veronica sipped from her glass, and looked at her over the rim. 'But does he know that?'

Kate looked uncomfortable. 'Well . . . '

'He's been kicking his heels around here, when I imagine he has more important things to do back in London. Don't you think you should make the position clear?'

'Yes,' sighed Kate. 'You're quite right of course.' She hadn't been fair to Evan. She knew it. Perhaps she had been hanging on to him as a sop to her self-respect, just for the knowledge that somebody wanted her.

'If it's not Evan you're mooning over, then it's some other man. What about the one who rescued you? Matt Selby. All that time alone with a man like that?'

'Mother!'

To Kate's relief George arrived carrying fresh drinks. Now perhaps she could sidetrack her mother's questioning, but Veronica had one further shot in her locker.

'Don't forget Evan is coming to dinner,' she said meaningfully taking her glass from the tray. 'I'm sure you'll both have a lot to talk over.'

But, later, Kate found it impossible to talk to Evan. It was a pleasant evening, relaxed and informal, but it wasn't the place for the explanations she felt she had to make. She needed to get onto more professional ground. Back to where they were only artist and agent.

'I was thinking,' she said casually. 'I must close down the exhibition.'

Evan demurred. 'Why not let it run, it's doing so well.'

'I really don't think there's much point,' said Kate. 'Most of the paintings have been sold, thanks to the recent publicity.' She pulled a face. 'I would rather they'd been taken on merit.'

'Don't be silly, dear.' Her mother sprang to her defence. 'I'm sure they've *all* sold on merit. I know I would have liked to buy them all.'

'You're prejudiced!' smiled Kate. 'And I'll have to pack up the remains of my things from the flat, and hand over the key.' She turned to Evan.

'You'll come with me, though, won't you? I expect you're wanting to get back to London. You've wasted enough time on my behalf.'

Evan raised an eyebrow. 'Yes, I'll come.'

'You . . . will come back?' asked Veronica.

Her expression was wistful, and impulsively Kate stretched over and patted her mother's hand. 'Of course I will. This is my home now. The only home I have.'

* * *

Kate enjoyed the bustle of Sydney. At least there was plenty to take her mind off things. She felt on neutral ground, more at ease with Evan, ready to pick the time and place in which to shatter his hopes, as she knew she must.

They enjoyed a little window-shopping, and a last minute tour of the bits of Sydney Kate liked best, from the iron lace-worked houses in the Paddington area, to the Harbour Bridge. The bold design of the Opera House mimicked the fat-bellied spinnakers of the sailing boats scudding about near Circular Quay. Kate enjoyed it, knowing that some time soon her mother would be broaching the subject of returning to London.

They took a taxi to the gallery. In spite of arriving without prior warning, they were enthusiastically met by the staff. Evan showed off, taking her around the remains of the exhibition, which had now been moved into one small section, pointing out how few paintings remained unsold.

'That's publicity for you,' he crowed, as if he could take all the credit.

'I would rather have done without it,' murmured Kate.

He gave her a sideways glance. 'I'm sorry. I know how that must have sounded, but I can't pretend that professionally I'm not pleased. And you'll have made a pretty penny too,' he added, almost as an afterthought.

'Then I shouldn't complain,' smiled Kate. No use being touchy. Certainly she was glad she had sold so much of her work. She would not need to worry about money for a while.

'The gallery will have the remaining paintings packed up properly for you,' said Evan. 'Where shall I tell them to send them?'

Kate thought for a moment. She supposed she would be staying, at least for some time. There would come a moment when she must leave, and pick up the threads of her own life, her own independence, but for the moment she would stay with Veronica. She owed her that much. And besides, she didn't want too much time on her own at the moment. When you are alone, you tend to think too much, to remember . . .

It did not take long to settle things. They had paper-work to complete, and Kate found herself promising that she would return, when she was ready to launch her next book, with its accompanying paintings. When they left and walked down the broad steps of the building, she was tucking a fat cheque into her handbag.

'You're stopping at the flat tonight?' said Evan. He sounded tentative. Did he expect her to invite him to stay?

'Yes, I'll be packing up the rest of my things.'

'But . . . you will have dinner with me? Unless you have other plans, of course.'

It was what she had hoped he would say. It would be so much easier to talk to him that way. She had to be very tactful. She valued Evan's friendship.

'I would have been very disappointed if you hadn't asked me,' she said warmly. 'Let's call it a celebration . . . for the success of our business venture.'

'And your safe return,' he said softly. 'We mustn't forget that. I'll call for you about eight.'

That afternoon Kate packed up the remainder of her personal belongings, leaving out only enough for her needs that evening. The flat looked bare and impersonal, and contributed to a feeling of depression that had been growing for some time. There was nothing to eat, and so she popped out to the deli on the corner for a foil-wrapped hot chicken and coleslaw roll, and a carton of milk-shake.

Eating her snack on the balcony looking out across the city to the harbour, she wondered what she was going to say to Evan. How was she to put it? She had to do it as quickly and painlessly as possible. It wasn't fair to keep him on a string, just to take her mind off Matt. *Oh Matt, damn you!* She tipped the crumbs out onto the ledge of the balcony for the birds, and went inside.

Perhaps because she was not really looking forward to the evening ahead, she prepared with extra care. She took a cool shower, luxuriating in the creamy feel of the soap on her skin, and thinking that never again would she take such mundane things for granted. Even when washing her hair she remembered how Taku had helped her tease out the tangles with a makeshift bamboo comb. It was as if that short time had become the most important time in her life. And yet it had only been a short episode. An interlude. And it was over. Forget it. Forget . . .

In the bedroom she had laid out fresh clothes, smooth silky undies that felt good to wear, and a smart black dress with a softly swirling skirt and a neckline that dipped at the back to reveal the smooth brown of her shoulder blades. She had lost weight, but not enough to bring angularity to her body, and if the face framed in that gorgeous halo of sherry-pale hair was a little finer, its cheekbones a little more pronounced, it only added to her appeal.

She snapped a silver bracelet around one slender wrist, and slipped her feet into sandals that had ridiculously high heels. Evan was a tall man, no need to fear dwarfing him.

Matt had been tall too. But *his* body had been hard and muscular, not soft. His shoulders had been broad, his skin brown, his chest shadowed with dark hair, where she had rested her head . . .

Kate found herself standing, as if in a trance, staring unseeing at herself in the dressing-table mirror. Her tear-darkened eyes stared back at her.

'This won't do!' she said aloud. 'It's got to stop.'

Restlessly she paced the flat, arguing with herself. Angry at her own weak will. What was she doing? Had she lost one obsession, only to replace it with another. Was that it? What had she expected from Matt Selby — that he should be madly in love with her? Wasn't that being naïve? Painfully she recalled a figure in a white jump-suit, with jet black hair. Matt wouldn't be lonely, of that she was sure. He wouldn't even be giving her another thought.

She sat on the bed, wrapping her arms around her body, rocking with her eyes closed, trying to ease the pain. How could she live without Matt? He was the only man . . . the only one who had broken through the protective wall she had built around herself. But that wasn't all. It was just being with him, loving him . . . needing him.

She was so thankful when Evan called for her that she greeted him with almost effusive warmth. He looked surprised, but pleased nevertheless.

'You look . . . well, stunning would be putting it mildly.'

'Thank you,' laughed Kate brightly. 'I'm sure you didn't think so when I stepped out of that helicopter at Wiatapi.'

'You never look anything but extremely attractive.'

She looked at him affectionately. He was certainly good for her ego, but that only made matters more difficult.

It was nice to be escorted, and taken care of. After a delicious meal they went on to a nightclub, Evan picking a table near the dance floor, not too near the band. He was a good dancer, leading her smoothly, his hand against the bare skin of her back, pressing her lightly to him. Kate allowed him to pull her close and rest his cheek against hers, but even close to him like this she felt nothing. The feel of another cheek invaded her mind, a cheek roughened with days' growth of beard, a mouth firm and insistent . . .

'D'you mind if we sit down?' she asked faintly.

'Of course not.' He guided her back to their table, and poured out another glass of the champagne he had ordered. 'To us,' he said smoothly.

'To our business relationship,' Kate countered.

He held her gaze and sighed. 'You can't blame me for trying.'

'I don't,' said Kate sincerely. 'I'm flattered.'

After that it was easier. The evening passed by pleasantly enough — and if her mind did stray it was because she found herself holding her breath every time a man went by who had dark hair, and that certain way of walking that made her think of jungle cats, and nights on a dark mountain when she had felt warm and secure in spite of the cold.

It was too easy to imagine she saw Matt everywhere. It kept her on edge, the sudden glimpse of a face, a mouth with lips firmly pressed, the way a man held a woman.

She tried not to look at the dancers, to keep her eyes on Evan, but in spite of herself found her gaze pulled back time and again to the other couples, the people at the tables . . .

And then she saw him! Her glass slipped from her fingers, tipped on its side, and the liquid shot in a stream straight into Evan's lap.

'Oh, I'm so sorry!'

But she could not tear her eyes away from a man who was sitting at a table in the far corner. Had it come to this, that she saw Matt everywhere? It couldn't be him, his face turned slightly away from her. But it was. He was sitting alone, staring at the long-stemmed glass he was holding between his fingers. He looked very different, so sophisticated in an evening suit that by its very cut shrieked out 'expensive'. He had shaved off his beard.

'It's all right,' said Evan. 'I'm only soaked.'

'Oh . . . good,' she said absently. She realised what she had said, and a wave of embarrassed crimson rose up her neck and into her cheeks. 'Evan, I really am so sorry . . . '

He had jumped from his seat, wiping the wine from himself with a handkerchief, but he too was looking across to the table where the man was sitting, alone.

'Isn't that the man who dragged you out of the jungle?'

Kate swallowed. 'Yes,' she said painfully. 'That's Matt Selby.'

Evan gave a short laugh. 'No need to tell me any more, Kate. It's written all over your face. You always did have an expressive face, you know.'

She made a small gesture of denial. 'Evan, I was simply surprised to see him here . . .'

'Come off it, Kate.' Evan sat down gingerly, hitching up the leg of his soaked trousers. He wagged a finger at her. 'I don't know what this is about, but I think you ought to go and speak to him.'

That roused her. Frightened her. 'No, I . . .'

'Why not? It would be churlish to ignore him, after all he did for you. Besides which, you've been irritable and on edge ever since you've been back, and it doesn't take a genius to see it has something to do with Mr Selby. I imagine there are things you still have to talk over with him. Well, here's your chance . . . he's on his own.'

'Evan, I can't — I'm with you.'

'My dear girl — I can hardly stay here with wet trousers! Now that you have a friend over there, I can leave you with a clear conscience. Goodbye Kate. I'll be hearing from you.'

She hardly noticed him leave. All her attention was drawn to that solitary figure. As if in a dream she rose to her feet, drawn towards him, half longing, half afraid. She skirted the edge of the dance floor, edging her way around the gyrating couples, and all the time he was half turned away from her. When she reached his table she stood behind him, nervously smoothing the material of her dress. She reached out a hand to touch him, and then withdrew. What was she doing here? Better to leave now, before he saw her.

'If you've something to say to me, you'd better sit down, Kate. You're in everyone's way, standing there.'

The words were curt, but his well-remembered voice brought such a rush of pleasure to her, that she took the chair he indicated almost without registering the fact that he sounded anything but welcoming.

He didn't look up, still playing with the stem of his glass. Kate licked her lips. Her throat felt dry and closed.

'You . . . knew I was there?'

He looked up then. A dark ironic look, a mocking smile tugging the corners of those well defined lips.

'I could hardly miss you. You've been circling the floor past me, you and lover boy, for the past five minutes.'

There was a bite in the way he said it, an echo of his anger at their last meeting in Wiatapi.

'I . . . didn't see *you*.'

He shrugged his shoulders, so broad under the smooth dark material of his suit. The very civilized nature of his clothing only emphasized that power he had always held, a primeval force that spelled danger. 'I'm not surprised,' he said with a stillness that sent prickles down her spine. 'You were far too engrossed. A fine couple you make, I must say. Very romantic. I was quite touched.'

She tried again. 'Matt, I wanted to explain . . . '

'There's nothing to explain.' He cut her short, his voice overriding hers. 'I hope you'll be very happy.'

Was he sneering at her? She flushed, her heart beating so loudly that she was surprised he could not hear it. 'You're determined not to let me explain, aren't you?' she retorted, stung by his attitude.

He looked surprised, his eyebrows raised. 'I doubt if I would be interested in anything you could tell me, Kate. As I remember it, you are too good at embroidering the truth.'

'I'm what?!' Her words had risen with indignation. She became aware that the people at the next table were staring, and lowered her voice, leaning forward, her hands flat on the table. 'And what do you mean by that?'

He leaned forward too, so that their faces were almost touching. She could smell the tang of aftershave, feel the warmth of his breath, and her stomach lurched with wanting him, but she managed to keep the wanting out of her eyes.

'I don't believe anybody would weep over me!' he mimicked savagely. '*Your* words, Kate. You spun me a proper tale.'

'All I told you was true,' she hissed, furious with him, with herself . . . and afraid. Oh, so afraid. Here she was with him, and she was wasting this chance. She was losing him. She felt it. Felt him drawing away from her with every passing second, and she could do nothing to stop it. Was hastening it, in fact. 'I told you things I'd never told anyone . . .'

'Oh yes, I believe that.' She could feel his eyes sweeping over her, mentally undressing her, and her lips parted as the melting inside her began yet again, but his words brought her to her senses.

'I don't doubt that you were one

mixed-up lady, Miss Summers. But there was one thing you didn't tell me. You didn't tell me you were engaged to be married.' Suddenly he leaned back, and folded his arms. His hair, she noticed, in spite of his immaculate appearance, was as shaggy as ever, falling forward over his forehead. He narrowed his eyes, staring at her in a calculating way. 'I suppose I should feel flattered that you chose me to have a little fun with. Didn't I come up to scratch?'

'How dare you!'

'I reckon I have the right!'

They were glaring at each other, she realized, as if they hated one another. *Oh God, don't let me mess this up!*

'You don't understand . . . '

Again he didn't let her finish. 'You're dead right I don't. I know the circumstances were, to put it mildly, unusual. But you didn't have to lie. You could have told me you had a fiancé . . . not all that rubbish about your past. Have you told him about us, Kate? Doesn't he mind?'

'But Matt, if you'd only let me . . . '

'You know,' he went on, steam-rollering over her as though she had not spoken. 'I don't like being used by a silly screwed-up woman . . .'

'Stop it!' She was on her feet, her hand swinging, but it never connected with his face. She should have remembered how fast his reactions were. He caught her by the wrist, his fingers curling around it cruelly, pulling it down, forcing her back into her seat.

'My, my. What a temper you still have, Kate.' His smile was icy, his mouth cruel. 'Not at all as cool and collected as you first appear. Now, don't you think you ought to go and find that fiancé of yours? I can't think what he is about, leaving you for all this time. But then perhaps he doesn't mind what you get up to — he's used to it. And I'm afraid I can't oblige this

214

time . . . I'm waiting for someone. Ah, here she comes.'

His eyes had slid past her, to someone across the room, and his smile had changed to one that was warm and welcoming. Instinctively Kate looked around. No white jump-suit this time, only a natty little number in scarlet, but the high cheekbones, the olive face, was the same. A flash of white teeth in an answering smile, and a hand raised in acknowledgement.

'You're right,' said Kate flatly. 'I should be getting back to Evan. Goodbye Matt.'

As she turned she thought he put out a restraining hand, but she did not look back. She steeled herself to walk away, her back proudly stiffened. Evan had long since gone. She would have to find her own way back. She retrieved her wrap from the cloakroom, and the doorman found her a taxi.

She reached the flat, still mercifully numb, and paid the man off. She let herself in, and switched on the light.

The place looked bare, as arid and unlived-in as her own heart. Even before she flung herself onto the bed, the tears were coursing down her cheeks, and the only sound to be heard was her own sobbing.

9

'But why are you going so soon?' Veronica padded around her daughter's bedroom, trying vainly to catch her attention. 'You've only just come, and now you want to go back to New Guinea. That God-forsaken place. Why do you want to go *there?*'

Kate folded a skirt and laid it neatly in her suitcase. 'Mother, it's not God-forsaken. Wiatapi is a very beautiful place. People travel from all over the world to holiday there.' She added a pair of sandals. 'And I have work to do.'

Her mind was made up. She needed to be alone to lick her wounds. And she needed to go back. The transition had been too abrupt, too traumatic. In the jungle she had found herself, and before she could come to terms with it, she had been whisked back here. She needed time. Time to look at herself. Time to get over Matt.

'But aren't you frightened? Of flying again, I mean?'

Kate gave a brief laugh. 'No, of course not. I flew back here, didn't I? I'll be quite all right. Don't fuss Mother, there's a dear.'

'Hmmm!'

Veronica sat on the edge of Kate's bed, and looked at her daughter. Kate avoided her eye. She knew her mother guessed that something had happened, and was worried about it. Her mother's next casual remark confirmed this.

'Evan's gone back to England then?'

Kate snapped shut the suitcase, and at last met her mother's glance. 'Yes, he has,' she said deliberately. 'And he *does* know the position. And we're the best of friends.'

Veronica nodded. 'I thought so,' she muttered vaguely.

Kate gave a wry smile. 'And am I to guess just what you mean by that?'

Veronica looked up. 'I'll show you,

dear. Come with me.'

Puzzled Kate followed as her mother swept out of the bedroom, along the corridor to the room that was now Kate's study. 'In here.'

Kate stood, mystified, looking around her. Her study looked just the same as when last she had worked in it. The portrait of Taku still stood on the easel. She would finish it when she came back.

'I must remember to take some pastels,' she murmured. 'And charcoal. I forgot that last time.'

'Never mind that.' Her mother crossed the room, and picked up a large folder that was leaning against the wall. 'While you were away I looked through your drawings.' She cast a quick defensive glance at Kate. 'I wasn't being nosy. Well . . . perhaps I was, but it didn't occur to me that anything might be private.'

Kate shifted uneasily. 'Of course there's nothing private . . . '

Her mother knelt down and laid

the folder on the floor. She turned the pages. 'What I found was very interesting. Lots of sketches, Kate. But they all seem to be of the same subject.'

She turned another page. 'Matt Selby, beating his way through the jungle, by the look of it. And this. Matt Selby, sitting huddled beside a camp fire. Matt Selby again, and this . . . and this . . . '

'Nothing strange in that,' said Kate, on the defensive. 'For quite a while he was the only person around. Why shouldn't I sketch him?'

'Oh, no reason, dear,' said Veronica softly. 'And then, of course, there's this one . . . '

She turned another page, revealing a large study of Matt. He was lying, naked and relaxed, on the mattress of leaves in the village hut. His head was slightly turned, his eyes closed. One arm was bent up behind his head, the other outflung in complete abandonment. One knee was drawn up, and there, where Kate had so tenderly placed it, lay the white orchid.

'Mother . . .' Kate's voice rose unevenly as she fought the constricting lump that had risen in her throat. 'I'm sorry if that one has shocked you. But all art classes use nude models. There's nothing so terrible in that.'

Veronica closed the book, and looked up at her daughter. Her eyes were gentle. 'Tush girl . . . you don't think I'd bother my head over that?' She beckoned Kate to join her on the floor, and as Kate did so Veronica put an arm around her shoulders. 'You've not had much of a mother these past years, my dear. But you've got one now. And I hate to see you unhappy.' She tapped the cover of the closed book. 'That picture was made by a woman in love. Deeply in love, Kate. I'd like to think you could tell me about it.'

With a gesture of surrender, Kate leaned her head on her mother's shoulder. 'There's not much to tell,' she said softly. And it was true. When all was said and done, if you put it into words it all sounded so stupid. The way Matt made her feel, that special understanding they had seemed to come to for such a brief time, it had all evaporated in the harsh light of everyday life.

'I think you know what a mess I was in after David. I couldn't get it out of my head that I was to blame. That because I had loved him, my father had died . . .'

'But Kate darling . . .'

Kate drew in a harsh breath, and lifted her hand. 'I know. I know how foolish it was, but that's how I felt all the same. I was afraid of men. Or, perhaps not so much of men, but of myself.' She shrugged, wearily. 'Well, I had to accept Matt. To survive I had to allow him close to me. Had to let him touch me. I came, well, I came to respect him, to trust him, and finally to love him. He gave me back something I had lost. I will always feel grateful to him.'

'Go on,' prompted Veronica gently.

'And how about him?'

Kate's smile was heart piercing. 'You mustn't blame Matt. I was silly, I suppose. I still hadn't grown up much. I thought it really meant something to him.'

'And are you so sure it did not?'

Kate shrugged. 'Quite sure,' she said bitterly. 'Matt was furious when Evan announced himself as my fiancé. He said I had been using him, had lied to him . . . but it wasn't because he cared, he made that quite clear.' She turned her head away to hide the tears that were threatening. 'Matt just can't stand lies.'

'But Kate, surely if you made him listen. Explained . . . '

Explained! Hadn't that been what she had tried to do in the night club in Sydney, but he hadn't given her a chance. He had flayed her with his tongue, the scorn in his eyes.

'It's too late for that. In any case, it seems that Matt had a commitment of his own. There's somebody else . . . '

The memory of that smiling brown face, that waving hand across the nightclub, seared across her aching brain. 'So you see, I just want to get away for a little while. I have to work. I *need* to work.'

Veronica drew her close in a fierce hug, and then jumped to her feet, suddenly brisk. 'Very well. In that case, let's get on with your packing. Charcoal, did you say . . . ?'

* * *

Returning to Wiatapi was, for some unaccountable reason, like going home. On the second day of Kate's arrival she entered the reception hall dressed in serviceable khaki shirt and slacks, her hair tied back, a knapsack on her shoulders, her folding easel tucked under one arm, a lightweight folding stool under the other.

'Going painting, Miss Summers?'

She smiled at the brown-faced man behind the desk. 'Yes, Kio. I thought

I'd work somewhere near the lake.' She hesitated. 'I won't be disturbed, will I?'

He answered her smile with a broader one of his own. 'No, Miss Summers. The others, they all go on trip today. Except the Major, and he never goes far.' He leaned forward, confidentially. 'He just sit on verandah with whisky dry.'

'Good.'

She left the Lodge, and crossed the open space of grass where the helicopter had landed. How long ago that seemed. She passed through the flowering shrubs, and on into the shade of the tall trees, to the narrow track that led away from the hotel. She was glad to hear that she would not be interrupted. She had already been introduced to her fellow visitors. A nice crowd, but she did not want their company now. And the Major would be safe enough. An old soldier, returning to the place where he had spent his time before the war, he wanted nothing better than to sit and dream.

Don't we all? she thought wistfully.

It was a stiff climb up the path that led to the lake, but easy walking compared with the trek she had undertaken with Matt. Would she ever be able to forget that, lay her memories aside, neatly folded and layered with lavender? Maybe, some day. But not yet.

The air was fragrant with elusive perfume, still except for the raucous, echoing cries of birds. She reached her favourite spot, a small grassy clearing overlooking the dark water. There she set up her easel, and unpacked her materials. As she seated herself comfortably on her stool she became aware of a new sound, the drone of a light aircraft. The day's new arrivals. But they would be busy settling in; and would not bother her. She began to paint.

★ ★ ★

She had begun a study of Arutap, based on one of the quick sketches she had started at the village. It was coming on well, but her heart was not in it and after a while she laid it to one side. She cleaned her brushes and began again. Working swiftly, leaning forward, tongue caught between her teeth, the long paint-brush stabbing with a life of its own, Kate worked with feverish intensity. Slowly Matt's face began to take shape on the canvas. It was a relief to give in to this driving obsession, to bring him back by recreating, as near as she was able, his face in every detail. His eyes looking back at her, dark, fathomless . . . as still as the lake. His broad cheekbones, betraying his ancestry, his lips full and clean-cut, firmly clamped together, his hair awry, filled with the same controlled vitality that was so characteristic of him.

Kate leaned back, and sighed. Would that she could exorcise through her art, this ache that pervaded her whole being. If only she could paint it away, rid herself of him. And yet, that was the last thing she wanted. No matter what the future held in store, she never wanted to forget Matt Selby, would not be able to forget him. He had become so much a part of her. If she were ever to forget him, she would lose herself.

She gazed back at the face she had conjured up, with a yearning that made her feel weak, as though the life-blood were draining from her very veins. Her blue eyes misted with tears. 'Oh Matt . . . ' she murmured. 'Damn you! How I love you.'

So wrapped was she, in a cocoon of grief and loss, that it hardly registered when a white orchid flower fell onto the painting. It bounced over her shoulder, landing on Matt's features. Then it slid downwards, smudging the canvas slightly, and lodged on the cloth Kate had tucked at the bottom of her easel. She stared at it, blankly. Then bent and picked it up. A white orchid . . . just like the one . . . just like . . .

'Matt!'

She whirled around, his name a gasp of surprise on her parted lips.

'Matt?'

Then suddenly the stool was over-turned, and she was on her feet and confronting him, awkwardly brushing away the tears that had been spilling, unable to believe what she was now seeing. He was there. It really was him . . . so much more alive than her picture. So vibrant, so sternly dark as he stared back at her, accusingly.

'Kate . . .'

One step and his arms were around her, crushing her to him, his head swooping down, his face blocking out the light as his lips plundered hers.

Her whole body was trembling. She could not understand. Dared not even think. She was aware only of the pressure of his mouth on hers. She wound her arms around his neck, with a sob of relief, her eyes closed. She breathed in the familiar scent of him, pressing her body desperately closer to his as his arms tightened about her. He gave a sound that was almost a moan, deep in his throat. Then abruptly he jerked his mouth away from hers, and stared deep into her eyes.

'Why did you let me think you were engaged?'

He was looking furious, and yet exultant. Kate shook her head, bemused, her arms still tightly entwined around him, her face tilted up to his.

'But I didn't . . . I tried to tell you.'

'God, woman! Call that an explanation? All you had to say . . . ' his voice suddenly became soft, unaccountably unsure. 'All you had to say was, 'Matt, I love you'. Nothing else would have mattered.'

Kate caught her breath. She swallowed hard, and closed her eyes, the long lashes lying dark against her cheek.

'How did you know?' she asked faintly.

'Your mother.'

'Mother!' Her eyes shot open, her mouth round with astonishment. 'What d'you mean . . . ?'

He gave a rueful grin. 'Quite a lady, your mother. When she'd finished tearing me off a strip for making you miserable, she got round to telling me a few things . . . things you should have told me yourself.'

'But . . . how could I?' Now that the surprise was wearing off, she remembered other matters that needed explanation, not least his commitment in the shapely form of a woman whose dark good looks had been as vibrant as his own. 'I thought . . . well, I thought the memory of what . . . what happened in the forest might be an embarrassment to you.'

She would not look away from him. Would not lower her eyes to hide the way she felt about him, but a warm flush rose from her neck in a wave, colouring her face.

Now it was his turn to look surprised, his dark eyebrows shooting up to his shaggy hairline. 'And what made you think that?'

She felt like a specimen butterfly, pinned by his piercing black eyes. She wanted to squirm away, but he held her close, clamped against him in a grip of steel.

'Well . . . ' she stammered, 'your lady friend . . . '

'My . . . ?' Suddenly he threw back his head and bellowed with laughter. 'Oh, you mean Storm.'

Storm. Yes, she would be called something like that. She had that hidden vitality, the same animal magnetism that Matt possessed. Kate had felt it, had felt how right they were together. It was nothing to laugh about.

In a sudden reversal of her emotions, she became angry. 'Yes, that's precisely who I mean. And don't tell me you and . . . and Storm . . . are just good friends. I saw the way she looked at you, that time by the 'plane. She loves you, just as much as . . . ' She nearly said, Just as much as I do, but he did not give her time.

'Yes — she adores me,' he said

calmly. 'And that's OK by me, but it has nothing to do with us.'

'Nothing! My God, Matt Selby, you like to have your cake and eat it, don't you?'

With one of his quick unexpected movements he bent and scooped her into his arms. For a moment the treetops spun above her, as Matt stalked off, pushing his way through the bushes.

'Put me down. Matt, where are you going?' she protested, all too aware of his face so close to hers, one arm around her waist, the other under her knees.

'Somewhere a little private. In case anyone comes along.' In a grassy clearing, he laid her down. The undergrowth was so thick around them that they might have been in a small private room, the grass a brilliant carpet beneath them, the sky a deep blue ceiling far above. He lowered himself beside her until he was leaning on one elbow looking down at her, his head blotting out the sun. Her senses began to reel, all the small voices telling her that she was being a fool, drowned by the surge of excitement that was making her tremble.

'If you're going to imagine things about every woman who hangs around me, you're going to have a pretty miserable time once we're married.'

She could hardly believe her ears. 'Married . . . but Matt, you've never asked . . . '

'You talk too much,' he growled, and then his mouth silenced her.

Why I am protesting? she wondered. She was being a fool again. Whatever he felt about Storm, or Storm felt about him, there was no doubt about what he wanted at this moment, he was making that abundantly clear. And she had to trust him. He would not have come to her, she now knew, if he was not free to do so. Her doubts melted away, as he covered her face with tiny feather-light kisses, sending a shudder of anticipation down her spine.

Gently he unbuttoned her shirt, and felt beneath her to unclasp her bra. With a murmur of appreciation he lowered his mouth to claim each burgeoning tip, cupping her breasts in his hands. Kate cradled his head, stroking his hair, and a shaft of joy so intense that it was almost sadness sped through her.

'Matt,' she murmured tremulously. 'You didn't have to come, you know. Whatever Mother told you. You owe me nothing.'

He shook his head in disbelief. 'What's the matter with you, girl? Is it still so hard for you to believe that a man wants you?'

He placed his face so close to hers that Kate could not focus on him, his voice purring in her ear. 'I want you, Kate. I knew it from the moment I saw you, before we got on that damned plane. I tried to fight it. I didn't want it. I told myself you were nothing but a nuisance . . .'

She made a gasp of amusement.

'And so I was . . . '

'No . . . ' he murmured, stroking back her hair, and nuzzling into the bend of her neck. 'Not to me. Never to me. You were . . . are . . . a stubborn, brave, foolish, adorable, mixed-up . . . '

'Mixed-up! Yes, I was certainly that,' she said breathlessly.

He turned his attention to her lips, tracing them with his finger, touching them gently with his own. 'At first I didn't understand. Then, after you saved my life . . . '

'But I didn't . . . '

'Don't interrupt. When you saved my life, and you came to me in the hut in the village . . . '

'I was shameless.'

'Yes you were, I'm glad to say.' He drew his head back a little, and she could see his face creased in a broad grin of reminiscence, his eyes gently mocking her. 'But then, I wondered if perhaps it was something you needed. Something to make you get over the past, and I told myself I should be proud if I could help.'

'But Matt . . . I . . . '

He stopped her with a finger over her lips. 'Hush now. Let me finish. This is something that needs to be said. I thought I could be noble about it, but then we were rescued and Evan turned up, claiming you.' His voice turned to a growl, 'I didn't feel noble at all. I felt bloody furious!'

'Evan only wanted to help. He never meant anything . . . '

'I know now. But I didn't then. I thought I'd been a fool. I'd let you get through to me in a way no woman ever had before. I'd been careful, you see. I'd not wanted any commitments, not with my work taking me all over the world. I thought there was plenty of time.'

Kate smoothed a dark lock of hair from his eyes. 'Was there never anyone?'

'Once . . . a long time ago. I thought we were to be married. But she didn't like my work taking me away. She was bored. I found there were other men. I couldn't take that. I'm a one-woman man, Kate.'

She smiled up at him. 'I'm glad,' she breathed.

'I hadn't meant to feel like this about anyone,' he continued, 'and when I thought you had been playing with me . . . '

Kate laid a finger on his lips. 'I fought it too, you know. I knew from the start that you were dangerous to my peace of mind. Disturbing. Unpredictable. That's why I was suspicious of you. I told myself I didn't like you. And then . . . and then . . . '

'Say it,' he urged.

Kate took a deep breath. 'I discovered I loved you.'

'Kate!'

They came together as a man and a woman should, with honesty, and delight. Kate felt as though she were riding on wings of joy, sure of herself, and proud, and willing. She answered Matt's caresses with her own, delighting in the sight of him, the feel and touch of his body, the taste of his mouth. There was no need to rush things, the time for that was over now.

'Oh, my darling,' she murmured, giving herself up to the wonder of the sensations that were coursing through her, pulling him close, opening up to him without fear.

'Always,' he responded. 'Always yours, Kate. As you are mine . . . always.'

Then there was no need for words, and pleasure turned into passion that made her move instinctively under him, arching against him, moaning as his fingers curled into her hair and the thrust of his body drove her to a place where she could not think coherently. Thoughts simply fled; she was conscious only of him, wanting him to continue, begging for more . . .

He knew her so well, so intimately — as though they had been lovers for a lifetime — and he used that knowledge to bring her to a peak of experience, so intense that it was almost more than she could bear. And then, when she cried out in instinctive protest, he held back, controlling his own desires to give her time. Kate opened her eyes, to find him looking at her with such tenderness that she caught her breath. What a man this was . . . so willing to give, so willing to put her before himself!

She reached up to him, curling her arms around his neck, searching for his mouth with her own, her body cleaving to his. How different this was from that wild reckless abandon by the waterfall . . . and even in the hut. Then she had set out to prove something to herself, and to him — had set out to make love to him, deliberately. But now . . . ah, now they had become equal. She could receive, and she could give, and it was her pleasure and delight.

'Now!' she murmured throatily. 'Now, Matt . . . ' Kate opened her eyes, and looked at the dizzy heights of the trees touching the brilliant sky. She moved, and nuzzled closer against Matt. He gave a purr of appreciation, and she kissed him lightly on the shoulder. He moved his head, pressing his lips against her hair.

Had he really said that . . . about getting married? It was hard to believe, and yet she *had* heard those words. She knew she had, but she scarcely dared to believe her own ears.

'Matt . . . ' she whispered.

'Mmmm?'

He looked so sleepy, so content, she hardly liked to disturb him. Perhaps it did not matter. If he had meant it he would say something sooner or later. If he had not . . . well, she did not want to think about that.

'Go on, girl,' said Matt. 'What's bothering you now?'

It was hard to find the words. She felt embarrassed. He raised himself on one shoulder, and she thought again with delight what a perfect specimen of manhood he was. She ran her fingers down his chest. 'I was just thinking how attractive you are . . . and virile!'

He raised his eyebrows. 'No you weren't. I know you, Kate. You hate untidy ends. You were thinking about what I said about getting married, weren't you?'

She would never be able to have secrets from him. She was glad about that. 'What if I was?' she teased. 'It isn't every day I get a proposal. If that is what it was.'

'Are *you* sure?' he asked, suddenly serious. 'You know how it will be. Sometimes you will be able to travel with me, but other times I shall be away for weeks . . .'

'Good. Then I can get on with my own work without interruption! You don't think I can manage without you?'

'You minx!' He rolled her on top of him, her hair falling forward around them. 'At least, it will give you the opportunity to be with your mother at times.'

Yes. She needed that. She needed space to continue her own career, to be her own person, and to come to terms with finding her mother. And Veronica needed it too. 'So it should all work out very well,' mused Kate aloud. 'Except . . . ' Ah yes, there it was again, that one little thought that would not leave her. 'Except . . . there's Storm.'

She held her breath, waiting to see his eyes cloud, any hint of evasion or guilt, but to her surprise the corners of his mouth began to rise.

'Yes, of course. She must be at the wedding.'

'Matt Selby!' Kate placed her hands on his chest, pushing herself up from him in outrage, but he held her around the waist, laughing — a devil in his eyes.

'Why not? After all, she's the only half-sister I've got.'

Half-sister. Of course. No wonder they had the same look of animal magnetism, that same lithe walk, the same turn of the head, quirk of the brow.

243

'Why didn't you tell me?' she breathed.

'Why didn't you tell me about Evan?' he countered.

'There wasn't really time.'

'Exactly.' He began stroking her hair, and a glow spread through her. 'There's a lot we have to learn about one another. But there's no hurry, Kate. We've got our whole lives ahead of us. And just at the moment, there are more important things to do . . .'

His arms tightened around her, and to her surprise she felt the hardening of his desire, and an answering flicker of fire in her loins.

'Not again . . . already?' she exclaimed in mock horror.

He chuckled. 'Don't be too sure. You're mine, Kate, and I'm going to make sure you know it. I love you, girl, and that can make me do extraordinary things, you'd better believe it.'

She knew what he meant, but she was thinking of other matters. Of the way he had half-dragged her, half-carried her at times, through the jungle. Of the way he had bullied, cajoled and tricked her into carrying on, when all she had wanted to do was sit down and die. Of the way he had tried to send her from him, when he had known the snakebite poison was working through him, in order that she might be saved. Of the way he had brought her back into the warmth of life as a woman, out of her cold dark obsession with the past.

She lowered her lips to his, and her voice was husky with emotion, knowing how much she loved him. 'I believe it,' she whispered, 'I believe it.'

THE END

We do hope that you have enjoyed reading this large print book.

Did you know that all of our titles are available for purchase?

We publish a wide range of high quality large print books including:

Romances, Mysteries, Classics, General Fiction, Non Fiction and Westerns.

Special interest titles available in large print are:

The Little Oxford Dictionary Music Book, Song Book Hymn Book, Service Book

Also available from us courtesy of Oxford University Press:

Young Readers' Dictionary (large print edition) Young Readers' Thesaurus (large print edition)

For further information or a free brochure, please contact us at:
Ulverscroft Large Print Books Ltd., The Green, Bradgate Road, Anstey, Leicester, LE7 7FU, England. Tel: (00 44) **0116 236 4325 Fax:** (00 44) **0116 234 0205**

Other titles in the
Linford Romance Library:

TO LOVE IN VAIN

Shirley Allen

When her father dies in a duel, Anna has no money to pay off his debts and is thrown into Newgate Gaol. However, she is freed by her cousin Julien, who takes her to her grandparents in France. Finding herself surrounded by people she cannot trust, Anna turns more and more to the handsome, caring Patrick St. Clair. Then, to her horror, she discovers her guardians are planning her marriage to a man of their choosing!

DREAM OF A DOCTOR

Lynne Collins

Melissa had discarded a sentimental dream of the attractive doctor who had inspired her to train as a nurse. However, his unexpected return to the hospital meant that she was constantly reminded of a fateful weekend. And so was Luke, for very different reasons. Time hadn't healed the damage done to his heart by her beautiful cousin, Julie, who Melissa knew he still loved. So it would be foolish to allow a dream to be revived when it could never come true.

SHELTER FROM THE STORM

Christina Green

Kim takes a job on Dartmoor, trying to hide from her unhappy past. Temporarily parted from her son, Roger, and among unfriendly country neighbours, Kim finds the loneliness of the moor threatening, especially when her new boss's girlfiend, Fiona, seems to recognize her. Again, Kim runs. But Neil, her employer, soon finds her. When Kim discovers that he, too, has a shadow in his past, she stays on at Badlake House, comes to terms with life, and finds happiness.

A SUMMER FOLLY

Peggy Loosemore Jones

Philippa Southcott was a very ambitious musician. When she gave a recital on her harp in the village church she met tall, dark-haired Alex Penfold, who had recently inherited the local Manor House, and couldn't get him out of her mind. Philippa didn't want anything or anyone to interfere with her career, least of all a man as disturbing as Alex, but keeping him at a distance turned out to be no easy matter!